The
Notebooks
of Leni Clare

The Notebooks of Leni Clare

AND
OTHER SHORT STORIES

By Sandy Boucher

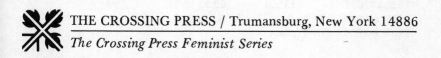
THE CROSSING PRESS / Trumansburg, New York 14886
The Crossing Press Feminist Series

"Kansas in the Spring" was first published in *Conditions: Four*, Spring 1979, then in *Lesbian Fiction: An Anthology* (Persephone Press, Watertown, Massachusetts).

"Nothing Safe in Crabtree Meadow" was first published in *Sinister Wisdom 6*, Summer 1978.

"The Day My Father Kicked Me Out" was first published in *Sinister Wisdom 14*, Summer 1980.

"Charm School" was first published in *The Bright Medusa*, then in *True To Life Adventure Stories, Vol. I* (Diana Press, Oakland, California).

Copyright © 1982 Sandy Boucher
The Crossing Press Feminist Series

Book and cover design by Mary A. Scott
Front cover photograph by Barbara Adams
Photograph of Sandy Boucher by Lucy Phenix
Typesetting by Martha J. Waters

Printed in the U.S.A.

Library of Congress Cataloging in Publication Data

Boucher, Sandy.
    The notebooks of Leni Clare, and other short stories.

    (The Crossing Press feminist series)
    Contents: Kansas in the spring -- Me and Ahnie Silver
-- Nothing safe in Crabtree Meadow -- [etc.]
    I. Title.   II. Series.
PS3552.'827N6   813'.54   82-2542
ISBN 0-89594-077-9   AACR2
ISBN 0-89594-076-0 (pbk.)

For Ann,
who may one day tell
her side of the story.

ACKNOWLEDGMENTS

I take this opportunity to thank some women who have believed in my writing and have helped me, in very concrete ways, over the years, to pursue it. My gratitude to Ann Hershey, Melanie Kaye, Forest, Tillie Olsen, Mary Wayne, Ms. Clawdy, Nancy K. Bereano, Lucy Phenix, Snake.

Contents

Kansas
in the Spring*

I

On Easter morning we drive out across the countryside until we arrive at a low concrete block structure painted pale green. On a bench next to the front door sits a young man in overalls, his skinny knees pressed tight together, his face knotting with anxiety as he watches us get out of the car. Arlyn speaks gently to him. "How you doin'? Windy out here, eh?" And the young man's face smoothes in a grateful childish smile.

This is the rest home where we will visit Bess, Arlyn's sister. Bess was the favored child in the family—a plump young woman grinning saucily out of the photographs. Her hair was fastened with tortoise shell combs into smooth dark cones and buns;

*This story was the beginning of my thinking about midwestern women that issued in the book *Heartwomen* (Harper and Row, 1982). A revised portion of "Kansas in the Spring" appears as the chapter "Amanda" in that book.

she wore silks under a fur coat. They sent her to college to be a home economics teacher. But something happened away at college. Aryln doesn't know exactly what. Bess was sent home. She became very strange, and no one spoke anymore of her teaching. For the next fifty years she stayed out there on the farm where she had to be taken care of by Arlyn and his other sister Emmeline, until Emmeline died.

Bess turns to us as we enter the dayroom. Hers is the same pouchy pink face as Arlyn's, with eyes of China blue. Her white hair falls down snowy and straight next to her cheeks. "Oh I am so glad you came," she says.

She asks our names, repeats them to herself, clasps our hands. She leans toward me, murmuring, "I am so glad to see you, Sandy," and her eyes are like those of a lover, so open and tender, so hungry. Sitting with her, I feel the wild fluttering of her being, the uncontrolled energy that might tip her in any direction. She is aware of the dangers; she hesitates often. It is like being with someone on acid, knowing that each thing I say goes through many transmutations in her head.

Now she must repeat the names again, asking for the surnames this time, spelling them, nodding with satisfaction when she has mastered each one. Her voice is an odd monotone like the sounds from a phonograph record that turns too slowly, the needle dragging.

"Bauer," she says, holding Mary's gaze. "B-a-u-e-r, is that right?"

"Yes," Mary answers.

"Mary Bauer," Bess repeats, her eyes dreamy, and then she slips away, her face suddenly empty of all expression.

Arlyn sits turning his cap on his knee. He has told us he does not understand Bess; she refused to help with the farm work or care about farming. He blames her for that. And he cannot quite forgive her for throwing away her chance to become a teacher, when she might have made a salary that would have helped them out during the terrible hard times of the Depression. So he is uneasy in her presence. But this place itself makes him uncomfortable, for some of the townspeople tried to get him committed here last year, and he had to fight for his freedom.

He sits staring at the floor, and glances up in exquisite discomfort when one of the old people in the room speaks to him.
Many of them here, like Bess, are younger than he; some lived
their whole lives in a neighboring town, on a neighboring farm,
known to him, but he maintains his stubborn separateness from
them.

Este has brought the still camera (we would never have dared
to bring either of the movie cameras), and now she asks, "May
I take a picture of you, Bess? I could send it to you later."

Bess rouses herself, looks at Este for a time as Este holds up
the camera for her to see. She nods. "Oh yes, you can do that
for me. I've been wanting my picture—the one from the Pledge
commercial. If you could get that for me. . . Yes, I'd be grateful. You know, it's me in the Pledge commercial, where I'm pol-
ishing the table. I'd like that one."

Este's expression does not change, but I notice the skin tight-
en around her eyes. Slowly she lowers the camera to her lap.

All Ann's efforts to coax Bess into talking about her past have
failed, leaving Ann silent and perplexed, and the rest of us secretly amused, for we know about the miniature microphone
taped to Ann's middle finger inside her cupped hand, the cord
traveling up the sleeve of her shirt to the tiny tape recorder hidden in the inside pocket of her down jacket. We had helped her
make these preparations back at the house so that she could
steal an interview for the film.

Bess does remember Ann. When we entered, she greeted her
with her childhood name, Ann-Marie, but she refuses to talk
about those days back on the farm when the child, Ann, would
come to visit. She ignores Ann completely to turn all her attention to Mary, Este and me. She touches us, tells us again in that
one-tone throbbing voice how happy she is to see us, how she
hopes we'll come visit her again. She looks at us so intently it
seems she wants to memorize us.

I think of Genevieve, Arlyn's wife, her long years of illness,
her early death—Ann's father writing in a letter "I do believe
that if Genevieve had been blessed with good health to go with
her natural drive she could have given Arlyn leadership and direction and they could have had a really good life."

When so many survived, why were these two destroyed? Genevieve, after all, simply did what was expected of her, like the women in the cafe, saying, "No, see, we all got married. There never was anything else."

And Bess? They lied to her about the world; they coddled her and dressed her up fine and gave her airs, prepared her for destruction.

Arlyn endures. "I love life!" he declares. Genevieve is dead now twenty years. While Arlyn awakes each morning, enjoys his food, tells stories, visits his beloved cattle. Lives his stubborn unwashed eccentric existence in the midst of his fellow townspeople.

Once, speaking of her, he frowned and shook his head. "I never could please her," he said. "Hard as I tried, I never could please her."

It was so long ago.

After sitting through an Easter mass served by a visiting priest, we take our leave. "Come back again," Bess urges. "You, Mary Bauer, and you, Este Gardner, and you too, Sandy Boucher," still ignoring Ann, who stands awkwardly by. "We will," I promise, and then think, why did I say that? and try to find a way to make it be true—perhaps if Ann gets more funding and we come back in the fall to film the townspeople, perhaps. . . .

"Goodbye Arlyn," Bess says, her manner growing more formal. "Thank you for coming."

Ever the lady, even in this most distressed and desperately vulnerable state.

Outside the front door of the home, Arlyn takes a long relieved breath, squinting against the sunlight. We follow his waddling, humpty-dumpty figure to the car.

II

I have climbed partway up the ladder on the side of the windmill and cling dizzily there, my head thrown back, while far above me, filling my field of vision, the blades of the windmill spin in my direction. The whole structure seems to move back over me. Much as I try I cannot convince myself it is only the wheel that moves, that the wheel is anchored to the structure on which I stand, whose spindly metal legs were driven deep in Kansas soil little less than forty years ago and have not moved since, that this tapered frame of windmill, as seemingly brittle as the thinnest of dried bones propped here, may strain against its crisscrossed wires but does not run with the wind or fall before it. Here where I expected to stand still—an eye only, a sharp observer's eye behind the camera—instead I am carried off in this rushing, this uncontrolled movement and opening of that which I had long ago closed away.

There is a whirring sound, and an occasional snap. The blades of the wheel race madly. The wheel itself seems to flow across the sky as I look up at it. Just as the new wheat flows in the field, a tide of short bright-green blades merged in their motion and then separated in ripples and torrents. A wide green rushing broken by the brown strips of road, the high ground of pasture where the cows stand blinking their pink-rimmed eyes against the wind that lifts the hair on their backs in stiff whorls.

* * *

We come back from an afternoon of shooting out at Uncle Arlyn's farm, unload the equipment from the back of the stationwagon, and carry the boxes and tripod and equipment cases up the broken sidewalk, over the porch and into our rented house.

We are here in Morrisville, Kansas, in the early spring—an all-woman film crew from California—to make a movie about Ann Hershey's family. Ann's mother and Aunt Genevieve grew up here, children of a big joyful prosperous French family in a

house on Main Street. Her mother, Marie Comte Hershey, is
dead, having suffered for years, like Genevieve, from rheuma-
toid arthritis. The townspeople remember the two sisters as
carefree girls, show us photographs of them clowning on a step-
ladder, wearing bloomers in the line-up for the high school girls'
basketball team.

To the townsfolk, Ann, now 38 years old and an independent
filmmaker, is still "Marie's little girl," remembered for her visits
here when she was a child.

In the living room of our house, Este, camera assistant, sits on
the couch with her hands inside the black bag, unloading ex-
posed film from one of the magazines. Mary, sound woman, and
Ann sit on the floor with the Nagra tape recorder, playing back
a tape of Uncle Arlyn telling us how the old house used to look
when his mother was alive. I am at work on the production
notebook, filling in details.

"Take 4: Sync sound. Arlyn opening gate, approaching and
turning on windmill. Yellow road grader coming right to left on
road behind him.

"Take 5: Same, except for road grader.

"Take 6: Close-up of Arlyn turning on windmill. Sync.

"Take 7: Arlyn feeding dogs. Then throws bag over fence
with the other trash.

"Take 8: MOS of broken tractors and other junk in the field
around the house."

(MOS, Mary Bauer told me, stands for "without sound." The
term came from a German director, who of course said "mit-
out sound.")

Ann explains once again where the emphasis must be. "This
time around, it's Arlyn we have to get. He's eighty-one years old.
He might be dead when we come back in the fall."

"I would like to make a request," says Este. "Do you think
you could get him to take a bath?"

* * *

Arlyn Lundborg. Short, round old man in overalls and a
filthy yellow shirt fastened at the collar with a large safety pin.

On his feet he wears black high-top tennis shoes; on his head a brown, billed cap, but this he always removes when he comes inside, revealing a head covered with white stubble, just like his chin. His face is Santa Claus plump and ruddy; his little eyes are a bright pale blue, now innocent, now sly.

Ann remembers his kindness to her when she was a child. He had let her ride his old horse alone about the farm, in long summer days of freedom. He had laughed when she drank from the horse trough, had shown her how to care for the animals she loved. He had been the one grownup from her childhood whom she remembered treating her with respect.

For the last few years now Arlyn has lived in a dilapidated house in town. There is no bathroom or kitchen in his house, and few unbroken windows. He lives, essentially, in one front room. Out in the weedy yard several dogs are chained amid an astonishing welter of junk, tractors and wagons, four or five big old cars, four pickup trucks. "How come you have so many pickup trucks, Arlyn?" I asked him. "Well," he said, "if I take one of them out to the farm and get it stuck in the mud, I just leave it there and come back here and get another."

* * *

I'm sitting on a rusted refrigerator in the yard of the farm, waiting for Arlyn to arrive. The sun is falling; a bitter wind claws at my jacket. Cows moo hungrily. It's depressing out here. The ruin of Arlyn's life. The neglect. The debris. The shit.

Mary talks about how everything here is dying. This is a dying culture—the small farmer, the family farm. All the young people go off to bigger towns, get jobs. The land at Arlyn's farm is strewn with rusting broken machinery, dead animals, objects from the past.

The ancient siding of the house, warped away from its nails, all color and sap and life drained from it by the decades of weather, taps randomly, gently against itself in the wind. Inside the house a closet door creaks, a rag of dress squeaks on a hanger, singing to itself. There is almost no inside to this house now, all apertures torn or smashed or simply left open. The piano stands foot-deep in cow manure on the living room floor. The ivory of its keys curls up like the fingernails of a Chinese empress. All the small noises of the house are quietly indifferent—sounds of a ship becalmed and abandoned in this great flat land stretching out to a smear of color where the sky lifts up from beneath it.

In this house Arlyn lived with Genevieve. We have wandered through looking at the objects here. Old flat metal bedpans, an ordinary wooden straight chair with small wheels attached to its legs to make a wheelchair for Genevieve. The bedframe piled over with rags, boxes, rusted objects, jars, photographs, papers flapping in the wind. The broken mattress upstairs spills brittle yellow corn shucks. It is the beds which shock us most, their desolation arousing thoughts of the woman who lay suffering year after year, her body curling inward, in that house without electricity or running water.

Ann realizes that in those happy childhood visits she had known so little of what went on in this house. Even then, apparently, it had been full of trash and falling apart—once with a big hole in the floor—in winter. And Arlyn did not bother to fix it. Genevieve was crippled by then, sitting in a wheelchair. She was Catholic, saintly; on her face was a smile of sweetness and re-signation.

He who has seen the sufferings of men has seen nothing.
Let him look upon the sufferings of women.
                                                      —Victor Hugo

* * *

Ida, proprietress of the Morrisville Cafe, has invited us to dinner, *sans* Arlyn. Her two sisters and her niece will be there. Ann decides this is the time to record the women's side of what happened in this town back when Genevieve was alive.

That evening Este and I position the light stands across from the line of booths in the cafe. We tape the big reflector sheets to their stands. Cables are laid across the floor to the power sources. I help Mary tape the microphone to the ceiling, so that it will hang over the booth where the women will sit. We set up the tri-

pod, attach the camera, snap on a magazine of film. The two
black magazine boxes sit on the counter, ready. The place is
cluttered with equipment now; we can barely squeeze through.
Ida and her sisters and her niece observe this preparation with
anxious glances. Now everything must stop while Este plies her
light meter and we hook up a new battery to the camera, just in
case.

And then Ida is talking, haltingly at first, while she works at
the grill. She tells about her life after her husband left her. The
difficulty of supporting and caring for her six children by herself, when she started to run this cafe. Her operations over the
years. Major surgery more than once. "But the cafe always gave
me something to come back to."

Out in the booth, Ann begins to question the women about
Genevieve. "When Genevieve came back from California," says
one of the sisters, "when she had just married Arlyn, why she
was real good-lookin'. She was tall and I remember she wore a
white coat. She had real nice clothes and she looked nice."

"Yes, I remember that," Ida says. "Then I went off to Oregon
to live for some years, and when I came back, why, it was a
shame! I couldn't believe it was her. She was all bent over sideways and so crippled she could hardly walk—and the clothes she
had on, well, I don't want to say anything about them. But it
was a terrible sight."

The sister nods. "But over the years, for all she went through
out there on that farm—and I never went out there to see for myself—but for all she had to suffer out there, I'll say one thing for
her: she stuck with him!"

The second sister remembers, "When she came to town, no
matter how bad off she was, she always had that smile."

III

Our rented house dates from the 1890's. It is actually quite
small, but is, as Arlyn points out, "conspicuous," set by itself
on a lot a little out from the center of town, toward the grain
elevator and railroad tracks. Dormers are built out from each
window upstairs; on the first floor is a deep wraparound porch;
up on top, a tiny attic room.

Inside, the ceilings are high, and the place is a mixture of the
original finishing and the remodeling done since. Old heavy
woodwork, new cheap plywood paneling. Fluorescent lights in
the kitchen. A bathtub upstairs that takes an hour to fill. Heat
from a floor register in the dining room.

In the front room our camera and sound equipment hunches
around the walls and sprawls over the couch. Lightstands lean
like streetcorner loafers in the hallway. A battery belt coils
over the arm of one of the three chairs in the dining room.

My production notebooks rest on another of the chairs along
with my small library that is meant to be consolation and escape: Annie Dillard, *Pilgrim at Tinker Creek; Womenfriends,*
by Walton and Newton; *Kansas: The Prelude to the War for
the Union,* by Leverett Wilson Spring. The last, in its battered library binding, was published in 1885, and happened to be in my
apartment in San Francisco. I am of the literal cast of mind that
requires when coming to Kansas one ought to read a book about
Kansas. There would be some security in knowing how many
bushels of wheat the state produces annually, how many U.S.
presidents grew up here—these facts to place over my own more
immediate awareness of this Midwest. I know these people; my
aunts lived in such towns as this all their lives, my former husband's mother came from a Kansas farm town. She carried its
morality and its social expectations with her wherever she went.
Statistics, then: Morrisville is a town of one thousand inhabi-
tants. Uncle Arlyn is worth a quarter of a million dollars,
thusly: he owns five hundred acres of farm land, each worth
$500. On this land he has a herd of about one hundred fifty
cattle. It was for such numbers that I looked in the Kansas
book, but found instead the ugly story of the struggle between

the pro-slavery people (mainly from Missouri) and the abolition-
ists (mainly from New England) to colonize and control the
Kansas territory before the Civil War. Lies, violence, greed; the
fight over abolition in the Kansas territory was a disgusting,
shameful series of events.

* * *

After days of cold and even snow, one day the weather sur-
prises us with balmy spring warmth. We eat lunch in the kitchen.
Salad in a yellow plastic bowl we bought at the dry goods store,
a cheese omelet, beer. I tease Mary, babbling to keep my spirits
up. I choose Mary to tease because she is the most distant of
us, the most ascetic.

In the hour before we must get back to work, Mary goes out
to lie in the sun in the side yard. I follow her out, lie down
about ten feet from her. We had a discussion two days ago
about a book she was reading, which detailed the process of going crazy. Lying there on the prickly grass under the hot sun, I
ponder that. Finally I ask, "Have you ever felt on the edge of
insanity?"

Silence from Mary's direction. I become aware of the hum of
the grain elevator, the twitter of birds in the trees near the broken sidewalk.

Mary says from behind a frown, "I am trying to sleep."

Why am I so vastly lonely, lying here looking up at the scrolls
and curlicues of our house, the trees just coming to bud, the
lovely house across the street that looks as if it belongs in Southern France, with its Mansard roof and subtle greenish color like
the patina on bronze. It is the loneliness I felt growing up in
Ohio, as if I was locked away from the life I sought, that must
be more passionate than the one I lived, more full of meaning.

The land stretches out—the miles of wheat fields, of pasture,
of milo for feed. I seek out treasures like the house across the
street, like the definition of "milo" that I copied from the dic-
tionary. Americanization of a Bantu word, "maili." It is "any
of a group of grain sorghums with somewhat juicy stalks and
compact heads of white or yellow soft grains." How did this

word travel from the black tribes of equatorial and southern
Africa here to Kansas? I occupy my mind with such questions,
in defense, for that which I did not expect is beginning to happen to me. A wound is opening, an old wound, to reveal the
thing hidden deep inside. We grew our layers of denial over it;
we grew passivity like a covering of spongy fat, hoping it would
protect us. We became complicit with the lying. Here in the
heartland, the requirements have not changed. I lied to Bess in
the rest home. I said blithely, we'll be back.

IV

SCENE: 5   **LOCATION:** Cattle auction, county
This shot with the Bolex   seat
                                      SOUND ROLL: 18

PRODUCTION NOTES: Camera footage of animal pens, restaurant (sign on wall reads "Cowgirls need love too"), auction
hall from the audience, auction hall from the auctioneer's booth.

   This is an octagonal building, pine-panelled, with bleachers
surrounding the arena floor, rising step-fashion up its sides. The
animals are driven in clusters past the auctioneer's booth into the
central enclosure, where the bidding takes place. Then a cowboy
using a stick with a nail on the end, drives them out again and
closes the gate. Pigs squealing. Cows pissing noisily. The cowboy accidentally slams the gate on a pig's snout, and the pig is
imprisoned there, shrilling loudly in pain. When the animal is
released, it staggers away from the door, blood streaming from
its nostrils.
   "My god, now I know why I'm a vegetarian," Este mutters
beside me.
   Ann is on the other side of the arena with the Bolex. A much
smaller camera than the Eclair, it is easier to handle in a crowd-

ed situation like this one, but it cannot be synchronized with a tape recorder, so that she is shooting silent footage.

Mary, with the Nagra tape recorder slung on a strap over her shoulder, earphones on her ears and the long foam-covered mike held out before her, is getting "wild sound," the random noises going on around us. She is tall and thin, small-boned, delicate appearing. In her rimless glasses she can look grandmotherly or like a skinny bespectacled child.

Uncle Arlyn pays close attention to the babble of the auctioneer, peers intently at the animals. He tells me how the bidding is done. The farmers do not want each other to know who is bidding on what, so each bids covertly with a subtle gesture. A finger raised to a hatbrim, one leg crossed over the other, hand brushing nose—all the while they try to look as casual and indifferent as possible. The auctioneer and the cowboy in the ring must be constantly alert to catch these secret bids. As he sees each bid, the cowboy gives a great whoop.

It's fascinating trying to see who's doing what, while they try to hide it. The older men seem to be doing most of the bidding. They are in general more dominant: probably they have more land and more stock and more money. This is the patriarchy, seemingly intact. The hall is filled with farmers of French and Swedish stock. Many have their male children with them. There are very few women here (though there are two cowgirls working in the stalls), and no brown or black faces in the crowd around me. This is a tight community, held together generation after generation.

At first we had been uncertain how the farmers would react to our filming them, but we needn't have worried. The auction hall is so much their environment and they are in general having such a good time, that the presence of these "girls from California" with their cameras and other equipment is only another occasion for fun. "Watch out," yells a man when Ann aims the Bolex at his seat-mate, "you might break your camera!" That and other tired witticisms make the rounds. The men tease each other about looking good, ask Ann if she wants their phone numbers, and laughter ripples about the hall.

* * *

At the restaurant in the county seat where we eat lunch, Mary
happens to burp, and claps a hand to her chest. Arlyn, catching
this gesture, looks up at her from watery blue eyes. "I guess my
table manners aren't too good." "No, no," Mary explains, "I
just had to burp. It had nothing to do with you." It's clear he
doesn't believe her. The rest of us chime in, trying to help.
"She didn't mean anything, Arlyn."

He isn't sure. He is quite aware that the sensibilities of most
people are offended by his person, that his neighbors disapprove
of the junkyard in which he lives, that his miserliness is a town
joke. He suffers from these attitudes, yet it's clear he would
change no facet of his behavior to make himself more acceptable.
When approached on the subject he retreats into acute discomfort.

Ann tries to convince him to install electricity in his town
house. Arlyn becomes very ill at ease, his eyes looking hangdog
and suspicious.

"But if you had electricity, you could have a television and
you could watch the baseball games," Ann says.

Arlyn shifts in his seat. "Uh. . .no. . .the wiring's bad. . .it'd
have to be all rewired. . . ."

"But wouldn't that be worth it?" Ann asks. "Then you
wouldn't have to sit in the dark at night, and watching tv would
give you something to do."

"I listen on the radio," he mumbles, and now we can't even
see his eyes, he has receded so far. Finally his hand lifts to brush
awkwardly across his face. It is a hand like a club, deformed by
work—the knuckles swollen, the fingers twisted almost sideways
at the joints. All of us stare at that hand, behind which he hides
his embarrassment.

Only when we change the subject does he return to us. He
watches us warily for a time, then begins to participate once
again in the conversation and ends by telling a rousing story
about a farmer who got drunk and drove his tractor into the
pond on Arlyn's farm, in the middle of the day, and Arlyn had
to pull him out or he would've drowned. And he laughs at his
own story, glancing around at us. Now he is innocent as a child,
his eyes mischievous and shining.

When we get up to go, Arlyn scoops the chicken bones from the plates and without bothering to wrap them, shoves them into the pocket of his corduroy coat. "I'm takin' these for the dogs," he explains.

"But Arlyn," I ask him, worried, "isn't it bad to give chicken bones to dogs?"

He nods good humoredly at me. "Well, they say so. You betcha they do. They say they can puncture their stomachs, but I've never had it happen." And he walks ahead of me out the door of the restaurant, wiping the chicken grease from his fingers onto his overalls.

* * *

SCENE: 7   LOCATION: Cattle feeding,
CAMERA ROLL: 28   Arlyn's farm
STOCK: 7247   SOUND ROLL: 20
ASA: Normal
LENS: 10 mm
FILTER: no

PRODUCTION NOTES: Take 1—Este shooting from the road to get the sunset out across the flat fields of wheat.

Take 2—Este inside cab of Luke's truck—sync sound. (Luke is the man Arlyn employs to feed the cattle now that Arlyn is too old to do it himself.)

Take 3—Este riding in back of truck—sync.

The cattle feeding is exhilarating to film, out in the cold wind just at sunset, bumping along in the back of a truck. At Arlyn's house in town, Luke and his son Kledis load thirty-five bales of hay and two bags of protein pellets onto the back of Luke's pickup. Then, with us following, they drive out to the farm, un-latch the gate and go past the dilapidated house into the open field. The cattle see them coming, begin to low and hurry to-ward the truck. Luke drives very slowly over the ground, which is bumpy with prairie dog holes, while in the back of the truck Kledis opens the bags of pellets and strews them on the ground.

The cattle have gathered into a great stumbling herd behind the truck, pushing each other, jockeying for position, leaning to eat the pellets. There are many new calves—wobbly-legged and curious, a bright redbrown, with white faces—who stumble in the midst of the hurrying grown-up cows and somehow never get knocked down.

Now Kledis begins to drop the hay behind the truck. First he cuts the twine holding the bale together, then lets the bale flake off and fall to the ground, where the cows begin to eat. There are two horses in among the cows: one runs around the edge of the crush, its mane lifting in the wind, looking wild and free.

Ann has agreed to let Este shoot the cattle feeding this time. (We will come back several times more to make sure we get it.) We have strapped the bodypod to Este's waist and shoulder and have attached the big heavy Eclair camera to the bodypod. Then we helped her up into the back of the truck where she braces herself on the tailgate, trying to hold the camera steady and stay out of Kledis's way, trying not to be knocked off by the cows who crowd up against the truck. Mary runs beside the truck with the Nagra to get sync sound, and I run behind Mary in case she needs me.

All this is very hard work and tremendous fun. I carry the magazine boxes and the filters and the production notebook. The weather has turned cold again. The wind is icy, and even wearing long underwear, two sweaters and a down jacket, plus a wool hat and scarf, and gloves, I must keep moving to stay warm.

When all the hay has been dropped from the back of the truck, we look out to where more than a hundred cattle are scattered in a long waving line across the land, their heads lowered to the hay strewn on the ground. Behind them, the sky has turned vermilion.

V

From the bathroom window I can see out across the open field to the grain elevator. In fact that's just about all I can see—that great high rounded building filling the space within the windowframe. Just beyond it is the railroad track, some scraggly trees. Now and then a train comes clacking along the track, screeches to a stop on a separate little side track near the elevator; a chute is moved into position, and the contents of the elevator slide down into the boxcars of the train. One by one they clang into position to receive their cargo. So all the way across the great flat central plains, each tiny farm town has its grain elevator on the railroad track, and the freight trains snake their way across, picking up the crops grown by the farmers and taking them to the big cities. Who in New York or San Francisco ever thinks about this vast flat land where the wheat for their daily bread is grown? I sit gazing out the window, a book open on my knees. The grain elevator, usually so monumentally silent, today emits the low roar of machinery. Not a soothing sound like the ocean or even the flow of traffic on a highway, that you live with and forget most of the time—this is a factory noise, whine of metal on metal, loud thumps and groans of weight being moved. It invades our house. I think of how it would be to live here as a wife and mother, caught in the house, surrounded by that noise.

The bathroom smells of mildew. I sit in here because of the little gas heater in the corner. On the wicker hamper under the window lies the Annie Dillard book, but the book open on my lap is called *Womenfriends: A Soap Opera*. It is a series of communications between two women who have been friends since college—a dual journal over a period of several years examining the development of their friendship. Pauline, college instructor and political lesbian. Rebecca, working woman, wife and eventually mother. Reading, I am often annoyed at the extreme self-absorption of these women, their competitiveness, their endless self-examination; yet at other moments I am won by their willingness to expose those parts of themselves which are least

attractive, to risk making of their friendship a process of
discovery.

But now in the quiet afternoon here in our rented house, under the roar of the grain elevator, with the little town spaced
out in yards and houses around me, and the vast flat empty land
beyond, I find the writings of these two articulate women as
foreign as, for instance, would be a Mexican restaurant on the
main street of Morrisville. Pauline and Rebecca live in the lar-
gest, most densely populated, most sophisticated city in this
country. The thoughts expressed by them come out of who
they are in that particular New York City environment, the relationship itself is one that would probably exist only among
sidewalks and subways and artists' lofts and expensive cramped
apartments. That women should be ego-centered and intensely
questioning, seeking full intellectual lives and professional ful-
fillment for themselves, *as well as,* in Rebecca's case, the raising
of a child—this would be heresy indeed in Morrisville. And that
there are women like Pauline who love other women to the ex-
clusion of men—well, that would call down the fury of these
Kansas patriarchs.

The independent women who surely existed in frontier
times—the entrepreneurs and adventurers, the scratchy cantan-
kerous separate women—their history is not felt in Morrisville.
The ones who surely exist right now are not visible here. And
yet the ideas of options for women are seeping out even here to
the prairie. Listen to this interchange from our evening at Ida's
cafe.

Jackie-Lyn, Ida's niece, who is in her twenties and the mother
of two children, asks of her mother and aunts: "Did it ever
cross any of your minds though, that you would ever be anything other than a wife and mother? Did you believe that was
your role? Your destination?"

They answer in a jumble, all talking at once: "There never
was anything else. . ." "No, see, we all got married." "You
have to take what comes in life." "Who had the time to sit
around making decisions?"

Jackie-Lynn: "Take girls today just coming out of high
school—they can go to college and they have a choice. They

can at least *think* about it. They may end up that way too, but
you guys didn't really have a choice."

"We did what we had to do," says the mother.

Jackie-Lynn (determinedly): "My daughter is real small now,
but as she grows up I'm going to let her know that she can be
anything she wants."

* * *

We are drawing close to Genevieve now, as surely our forbear
as if all of us, like Ann, were Marie's little girls. That big-fea-
tured face, long and skull-like with jutting nose, the dark eyes,
the black hair hanging straight to just below the ears. Genevieve
in her wheelchair, placed at center-front of the group at the family reunion. Wasted face gently smiling. Her body, bony and
contorted, leans sideways in the chair.

The women in the cafe speak of her suffering. First for arthritis, then later for cancer, she had sixteen operations. During
one early surgery something was left inside her body when the
incision was sewn up. They don't remember what exactly—a
pair of scissors? some packing? Its presence inside her caused
terrible complications. Later the surgeon opened her up again
and found it. Arlyn did not sue the doctors or try to get any
restitution from them. Genevieve simply endured.

On the days when we must film out at the farm, we stumble
about glum and angry. The wind whipping through the broken
windows of the house murmurs to us of Genevieve. What was it
like to come back from each surgery to this house without lights,
without a bathroom?

And the summers. Arlyn has never planted a tree. The house
has no shutter, awning, porch, and never did. It is a tall box
with gaping holes for door and windows. There would have
been no shade, no relief from the heat.

Yet the past is slippery. What can we *know* of Genevieve,
dead since 1952. Ann remembers a woman in a wheelchair.
Genevieve died when Este was only one year old, when Mary
was eight years old, Ann thirteen, I sixteen. So we arrive at her
from different historical perspectives (a fifties teenage was dif-

ferent in crucial respects from those years lived in the seventies)
and lifestyles (two of us are heterosexual, one now living with a
male lover; two of us are lesbians). But Genevieve is a wound
in all of us by now, torn open. Inside is found the object, the
perception, the anguish we thought we had buried or that we
never knew was there.

Arlyn told a story set in the Depression, a cruel time for him
and Genevieve: "Genevieve and I, we got started to, during the
hard times. . .we had her dad to take care of and we couldn't
and uh, work was scarce then, we had to do something! And
we'd go make these trash piles and pick out stuff to wear, shoes
and whatnot. You know, now Genevieve was, you might say,
raised in wealth. . .she was. . .and that was an awful comedown
for her. As a girl she had everything she wanted, about. . .she
wasn't forced to work and go off and make these trash piles,
that was quite a comedown for her. Well, one day Genevieve
and I were in the trash pile looking for things. The bus and
preacher came by and they stopped to see who it was, and he
saw it was us. Well, he just stuck his head up and drove on, like
he didn't even recognize us. And Genevieve says. . ." Arlyn
lifted up his head and laughed in admiration. "She says, 'Well,
go ahead, it doesn't matter to me, if that's the way. . .' She didn't
care who saw us."
  Ah she must've been a feisty one, we tell each other. She
must've given that Arlyn a hard time. But we have begun to per-
ceive the breadth and depth of Arlyn's stubbornness, this obdu-
racy slyly masked by the appearance of yielding. (How come
you never brought that piano into town when you left the farm?
Mary asked. Arlyn glanced at the ruined piano standing in its
layer of cow shit, and said serenely, Oh yeah, you bet, one day
I'm gonna do that. And he believes he *will*, while of course
having no intention of doing it.) So it comes to us that Genevieve, isolated out here with only Arlyn for company, had to
live *around* that immovability, had to make the best of what
little there was in that stark, barnlike house, of comfort, of
companionship.

Mary has a theory. "Think of the illness as resistance," she suggests. "If she was sick she couldn't breed; if she was crippled she couldn't work."

To resist by destroying oneself, to sacrifice one's body, is a gruesome idea, but it is better than the thought of Genevieve as passive victim with *no* control over her destiny.

—or "destination," as Jackie-Lynn put it.

(Excerpt from a letter from Ann's father):

"Arlyn came of old, basic Swedish farm stock. Stolid, unimaginative and rather insensitive. Never vicious, mean or cruel. . . . I suppose to Arlyn and the men of his family women simply endured the frailities of their lives. It was Genevieve's misfortune to have more than most to endure."

VI

SCENE: 10

CAMERA ROLLS: 25, 26, 27

STOCK: 7247

ASA: Normal

LENS: 9.5–95; 25 mm (cam roll 27)

FILTER: 85 (cam roll 26)

LOCATION: Barn sale, neighboring town

SOUND ROLLS: 19, 20

PRODUCTION NOTES: Begins with long shot of farm from the road; snow on red roof of barn; pickups and cars lining the road approaching farm.

Takes 1 through 6—auctioneers auctioning junk from a flatbed wagon. Arlyn in among the crush of farmers bidding for items and buying them.

Takes 7 and 8—Women inside barn, selling sandwiches and pies and coffee to the farmers coming in from the sale.

End of roll 26 is just outside the barn, where auction notices are tacked to the barn door. Men stand looking at the notices, which lift and flutter in the wind.

On the way to the sale, Arlyn explained. The owner was
giving up his farm to move elsewhere; probably he had already
sold it. Now he wanted to sell all his equipment and farm ve-
hicles, everything he had used to work with over the years.

In the back seat, as we drove out into the bleak snowy morning, Este and Ann and I sat crammed together, film gear piled
on our laps. I looked out across the open fields to the occasional lines of trees, wondering if Este and Ann were as aware as
I was of Arlyn's manure smell here in the closed car. When Este
reached to open the window a crack, I smiled.

At the sale, now, there is a sharp wind, and the two auctioneers at work up on the flatbed trucks among the piles of junk
are bundled up to the ears. Mud everywhere. Scattered snow.
The farmers with their bright billed caps—orange and yellow and
red and green—bearing the insignia of farm machinery companies and feed companies.

While Este and Mary and Ann are getting the equipment out
of the back of the station wagon, strapping the bodypod onto
Ann's shoulder, I retreat to the barn. Inside, a dozen women are
busily at work. Before them are board tables loaded with home-
made pies and sweetrolls, urns of coffee. Behind them are the
makings for ham sandwiches, barbecued beef, hotdogs.

The farmers stamp about the doorway, huddling half-in, half-
out, drinking coffee. A raw wind enters among them.

While I know I should hurry back out to help start the filming, there is something in this shadowy barn of much more urgency for me. I stand in a corner eating a piece of warm apple
pie, watching the women busily setting out the food. There is
not one woman here under the age of fifty. Their eyeglasses,
their headscarves, their thick wool coats draw my gaze; their
mouths are tight with all the years of doing what was necessary,
their eyes shy and curious behind the glasses, noticing me as a
stranger, even as I am feeling so much a part of them. I am so
relieved to be here among them. They can't know this. Possibly
they would not want it. Nor understand my affection for them,
how much I want to talk with them, come back in the fall to
hear their voices, let them speak their lives. And the cowgirls at

the auction hall, the waitresses in the cafes, the wives on the farms—that society of women hidden from us this time around.

I should go outside to help with the equipment; I know Ann will be impatient with me. But I am not yet ready to relinquish this good feeling. I want somehow to take it with me, and I think of the still camera I am carrying in my pocket. Yes, perhaps a picture.

When there is a lull in business, I approach the table. Will they let me photograph them all together, I ask, to the women in general. They look embarrassed. I tell them I am from California, I've never been to an event like this barn sale and I really want to have a picture of them, if they don't mind. There are some moments of hesitation, in which I feel ridiculous, aware of how conspicuous I have suddenly become. But then the women cluster together for the portrait. Looking through the viewfinder at the faces of these stolid survivors, I understand why Bess and Genevieve cannot be here, they who carried the weight of madness and pain.

Now I really must leave the barn and go out to help the others. The women return to work again, arranging food on the table, stirring the barbecued beef in the steamer, slicing the pies.

Outside, the wind is a knife ripping at my clothes. Across the barnyard I see the "girls from California," heavyladen with equipment, making their way through deep squishy mud toward the crowd of farmers around the flatbeds. I hurry to join them.

Me and Ahnie Silver

There was a sense of something missing, right from the beginning.
I felt the lack that first Sunday when she arrived at my house.
Sitting in my living room, Ahnie talked at length about her work.
"This fall maybe I should go ahead and do it," she said. "Really,
Columbus, Ohio is no place for a dancer. There's no stimula-
tion here. No challenge. People tell me I could do well in New
York. . . ." I watched her, speechless. Her perfect blondness,
her height, intimidated me.

"I like you as much today as I did last night," she said, and I
found her words hard to believe, for no particular warmth came
from her toward me. I was puzzled by her, until, when she got
up to leave, she stopped at the door and put her arms around
me. She held me with surprising urgency. When she pulled
away to leave, excitement welled up in me, and my questions of

24

a moment before drowned like helpless kittens in a flood of desire.

We were unlikely people to be together. Ahnie's dance classes and performances were attended by the young hip women in town; she was the darling of the lesbians and feminists up near the university. I live in the same house in Grandview where my family lived, and now, in my forties, I am still working at the insurance company where I started back when I finished high school.

Maybe we should never have made love (we moved so easily over into sensuality, and then sexuality), but the night it happened I did not feel it as a mistake. Our being there together seemed wondrous to me as her hands cradled my thighs, heartbreakingly gentle. Lingering, palms brushing my skin, she smoothed the fine hairs there. I lay absolutely still, responding to all the comforting I could ever have wanted.

I stroked Ahnie's pale straight hair. Her cheeks were flat above a squared chin, her mouth a straight line. Her skin was deeply sun-tanned, bronze on the shoulders and arms, red gold on the face. I was immensely intrigued by her face as it changed, when she was disturbed, clenching into a tight wrinkled scowl. When I held her, making love to her, she turned her head against my arm, eyes closed, sucking my skin in her excitement, not wanting to open her face to me, let me look deeply into her eyes. And I was so moved by the flat expanse of her cheek, the line of jaw, the lock of hair lying next to her ear, the muscles of her throat swelling under the tanned skin. I was touched by her hiding away from me in her desire.

She eluded me, from the beginning, even in our most intimate moments. It was like a chase: Ahnie glimpsed for an instant—Ah, there she is!—and then gone. I had had several wonderful lovers in my life, women who satisfied and instructed me; never had I been with someone like Ahnie.

Only in her performing was she fully present. Dancing, she projected a special quality of delight. She opened herself to her own magic when she was in public, with an audience, with students. The smile then—dazzling. And the eyes partook. They were extraordinary in that blond face, brows and lashes colorless so they startled in their pale clarity. Eyes full open and brilliant: she glowed. This gesture was immensely affecting, something of surrender in it. I watched the people gather about her after a performance—she taller than many of them, standing there in her white performance suit, the brown of her beautiful arms and shoulders deepened by the contrast. She clutched a bouquet to her chest, looking into the faces of her admirers, offering them her complete attention with that miraculous smile, those eyes saying, You are magical too. I acknowledge your being. A joyous love came from her, and they gathered about waiting to touch her, embrace her, smile into the full beaming of herself that she gave them

When her students discovered we were lovers, they said, "How wonderful!" "Ahnie Silver is so wonderful." They said, "She must be very easy to love." They said, "Ah, you're so lucky!" My old friends gazed curiously at me when they saw us together. I knew they were wondering what Rose Giannini was doing with someone like Ahnie. Most of them are securely settled in couples, own homes together, have raised each other's children and supported each other over the years. They wondered what Ahnie and I had to say to each other.

Her face was so often closed in worry when she was with me: she worried about money, her classes, her car, her big floppy afghan dog, Spark, who was silkily delicate and ridiculous and often sick. She worried about the aching of her legs, the dried flower arrangements on the walls of her apartment (Did I like them? Were they too impersonal? Should she hang posters?), the way her apartment smelled.

In fact I did dislike her place, in one of those cheap apartment houses thrown up for students right near the university. Her apartment was a sterile, white-walled box, and I could not understand how she could be so contented there.

She lay under the sun lamp's harsh light, saying, "I wish I had smooth arms like yours."

"But it's because my muscles aren't developed," I laughed, "and look, I'm getting flabby!" Lifting my arm to show her.

"No, most women's arms are like yours. Even if you developed muscles, your arms would be smooth."

"People are turned on by your muscles," I reminded her.

"I know. Now they are. A lot of women are now, because of the women's movement. And some men. But I used to be ashamed of my muscles. I wore sleeves to cover them up."

She had long legs, a tight round behind, absolutely flat belly, slim upper body rising to shoulders held a little forward, muscles of arms and shoulders boldly defined under the brown skin, muscles of back beautifully articulated.

I sat on her bed watching her as she lay under the lamp.

"I like your muscles, Ahnie, but I don't love you for your body."

"Yes, I know that." She turned to look at me. The smile that began was not the vivid, public one. It was thoughtful, for herself and for me.

Yet if I am honest, surely it was the romance of a perfect body, that physique in which she was more present than in her emotions or her spirit, that drew me. And I know I basked in the glamour of her performing, vicariously enjoying the applause.

In that first month I was swept with a consuming hunger for her. I remember the expansiveness, the charm, with which she turned toward me, the way she opened to me, questioned me about who I am, what I like, what I think—arrived on my lunch hour at work with sausage and pickles and tomatoes and pumpernickel so that we could eat together before she had to hurry off to teach a class. And when she came to my house late, after her classes were over, we ate dinner and she talked with such intensity about teaching, performing, about what was going on in the New York dance world, about her plans. I was dazzled by her, all of this new to me. Ahnie's life seemed so much more vibrant than mine, or, *crucial,* as if she lived closer to her own hot flame, so that each moment mattered. We stayed up until dawn sometimes, and often the next morning I went in to my job late or not at all. And Ahnie said, "Let's live together. I want to have a home with you." I did not know how to respond to that because it seemed she wanted to install herself in my life —to have me as support for her work, companion for her home life. My family's old house is really a home to me after all these

years: perhaps she felt she would be taken care of by me if she
moved in with me here. I was forty-three while she was not yet
thirty: was she looking to be mothered? I held back, cautious,
noncommital. But deep inside I was certain we would live together very soon, for I wanted a life-partner, one who would
daily share my existence. It's what I was used to. I had lived in
this house with a lover five of the seven years since my mother
died. That daily intimacy seems to me the most human way to
live.

So I perpetrated a fantasy. There was that gap in my life and
Ahnie would fill it, even though I suspected, from all the evi-
dence, that she was not a person to depend upon. I went right
ahead with the dream anyway, imagining Ahnie and I settled
in domestic bliss, letting the momentum of my desire carry me
forward.

One Saturday afternoon she arrived for a surprise visit, saying,
"Let's go upstairs and make love." And the very next day we
did it again, and she said in astonishment, "That's the first time
in my life I ever made love two afternoons in a row." I was
used to more voluptuousness in lovers. But Ahnie lived for her
career, anxiously tending the details of her work twenty-four
hours a day. She could not lie in bed in the mornings; she
went out to breakfast—to a restaurant where everyone knew her.
Sometimes I went with her. We drank strong coffee and talked
about her work. I learned from her. I was neglecting my own
work to be with her. I had no time anymore to spend with the
nieces and nephews who used to demand so much of me. I
made excuses to my sisters and their husbands when they invited
me over. I told my friends I was too busy to see them. All this
so I could be available when Ahnie needed me.

She began to withhold herself. She began to find fault. "You
are very needy," she said. "You are a subtly controlling person."
"You want more than I can give." "You want to consume me."
In the morning she lay rigidly separate and would not touch me.
I was confused then, feeling shut away from her; and her face
looked so angry that it seemed she was punishing me for something. I could not leave her apartment without asking, "Will you
hug me?" Her anger flashed out at me. "Why can't you allow

me my freedom!'' Until everything I did was seen as an attempt
to manipulate her.

We were making love: I unbuckled her watch, removed it,
placed it on the bedside table. Hours later, the rage boiled out.
"How dare you take off my watch! How dare you intrude on
me like that!" It had seemed so natural to me, thinking she had
forgotten the watch and I was doing her a favor by removing it.

"Why are you so angry with me?"

"Because I needed to be alone after dinner," she said. "I
wanted to go in the bedroom by myself for half an hour."

"Yes?"

"Now I feel smothered by you."

"But why *didn't* you go off by yourself after dinner. I would-
n't have cared."

"I don't know. I just didn't. I stayed talking with you."

"Do you want to be alone *now*?"

"No, it's too late now. I'm too angry."

At her work, Ahnie was always with students or audience, always observed, and when she left it she wanted to be alone.
Knowing my job so well, bored with it, I looked for stimulation
in my evenings and weekends. We conflicted. There were the
signals that she wanted to be taken care of: losing keys, losing
money, breaking things, leaving things, the distraction, the distress. And when I responded instinctively, moving forward to
help, she said it made her feel inadequate and controlled by me.
"Don't help me!" she snapped, "I don't want your help."

I knew it was wrong. Sometimes I talked to myself, saying,
Rose, you could stop this, you could step back, say I don't want
this. But there was such intoxication in some of our time together, as if we escaped real life, with all its responsibilities, to
become children again. I had let myself become addicted to
those moments, imagining they could make up for the rest.

At the studio where she taught and performed, she stepped
into the center of her power. Here she could afford any gener-
osity. The Silver Dance and Gymnastics Studio on High Street
near the Capitol looked like any other storefront from the outside, but inside a hardwood floor had been carefully laid, spot-
light racks hung high up against the walls. Ahnie had created

this environment through five years of discipline, effort, risk of
herself. Perhaps only here in all the world was she safe. In this
great high room with its wall of mirrors she was gracious, even
to me. She made a place for me here where I might have been
so at loose ends. I was her special person in the studio, lovingly
touched, asked for my opinion on her costume, how she should
begin, should she use the drum? And after the performance
when she stood still, letting the people come to her, speak to
her, touch her, I waited; until at some moment suddenly she
was there before me, grasping my arms, wanting me to touch
her, kiss her, wanting to know, Was it all right? Was I good?
Did I do well?

We went out to eat, then, with the money from the gate—a
few of her friends with us. In the Chinese restaurant, loud and
busy, she and I sat next to each other on the bench against the
wall, thighs touching, enjoying this closeness. I was exchanging
funny remarks with her friend, who sat across from us, and I
had a sense that now in this verbal play *I* was performing for
Ahnie. I could feel her pleasure in watching me.

Then, leaving the restaurant—it was near midnight—in the car
and in the kitchen of my house, she wanted to hear from me in
detail about the performance. I told her what I had seen; I
called up the parts I found most powerful or interesting. More
than that I could not tell her because I don't know about dance
or movement, how it should be. She said that's all rigid tradi-
tional bullshit anyway; what she wanted to know was what
happened inside me as I watched. I tried to tell her, searching
for the words that would name my feelings. I was secretly
thrilled by this sharing, experiencing an energy, almost a fervor,
that I remembered from my childhood.

When I was a little girl I had thought I would be an artist,
maybe the person who painted the statues in the church, or a
singer warbling *Ave Maria* so beautifully that everyone would
cry. My mother and my sisters and brothers and I spent so
much time in church that it was the theater for all my fantasies.
But out in the world, I always settled for what was practical,
taking the secretarial course in high school, working to put my
brothers through college. Then when Papa died, my sisters were

already married or engaged, and my brother was in medical school: there was no one else to take care of Mama and it was important not to lose the house in Grandview where we'd all grown up. So I stayed there with her, keeping my secretarial job at the insurance company, where eventually I was promoted to underwriter. But even after all those years of issuing insurance policies, the desire sometimes awoke in me to reach inside to what was most true in myself, bring it out and shape it as something in the world, the way Ahnie shapes her feelings into a performance.

Our merging was powerful—much of ourselves simply accessible to the other without effort on our part—to a depth that I have experienced with few others. Making love to her, that afternoon when she arrived to surprise me, I saw the insides of her thighs, her pubic hair. It seemed she was golden, the blond hairs on the tanned skin. A golden woman who was so fully present there with me, so without fear or defensiveness, not yielding so much as opening physically to my opening, that I was carried out in waves of feeling that can hardly be called pleasure. It was more a heaving, awakening of senses in my spine, my groin, capacities locked away even for years. I knew she experienced it too.

It was this wonderment and deep physical awareness that forged the commitment in me. I remember that flat voice speaking softly next to me in bed. I had turned to rest my closed eye on the curve of her shoulder, enjoying the warmth of her flesh against the skin of my eyelid. "You're very sweet," she murmured. And I who have sometimes in my life felt so ponderous, as if my flesh were stupid and slow, not worthy to be loved, experienced myself lithe and cherished.

At first there was such delight in discovery. I found that when I was not with her I was aware of walking like her, of making the gestures her body makes—that leaning forward, knees flexed, that attitude of listening, the head thrust forward and up. This mimicry became a pleasure I cultivated: talking to someone at work, I heard myself speaking with her inflection; I continued it, secretly playing this game of closeness with her while maintaining a perfectly reasonable conversation. Delicious. Walking

from the office building to the parking lot, I enlarged my stride
to adopt her vigorous athlete's walk.

How it comes in, now, the ways in which she held herself
away from me: remembrance of a morning at her apartment
when she was making love to me. I felt her strangely separate in
the act, hiding off in herself even as she stroked my breasts, bent
to kiss my throat, and I found myself staring at the photographs
of her taped to that stark white wall next to her bed. Ahnie,
seated among her dance students, looking sideways at them,
gesturing as she spoke. I stared at this picture—and next to it
the photo of a performance she had done in the nude, her body
supported by a group of dancers. Her hands stroked my belly,
her tongue moved delicately. I came back to her real self, to
touch her brown shoulders, her hair—but my eyes kept return-
ing to the photographs, seeking out those two images that could
give her to me. She lay her cheek against my belly, her voice
came, "So sweet." And I stared at the spread-open nude body
held ecstatically aloft, turned my eyes to the intent face of the
teacher speaking to her students. Hoping to know her in this
moment, touch her, I was caught in the space between those
cardboard images and the woman of flesh who lay cradling my
hips. In this most intimate of situations, Ahnie was strangely ab-
sent.

She was interested only in herself and her career, caught in
the habit of tight focus on a goal. The rest was worry: the elab-
orate fumbling ritual with her contact lenses. They did not fit
right. Were they scratched? Taking them out, washing them.
Were they lost? Dropped on the floor. Stuck to the side of the
bottle. Putting them on. Discomfort. The indecision over a
place to live. Move or not move? Go once and for all to New
York? There were problems with the car, and with Spark, who
was scratching a lot. He might have some kind of mange, and
what would she do about *that!* A favorite student did not come
to class. Was this a gesture of rejection? She lay for hours under the sun lamp, worrying. I saw how ill-suited we were for
each other, I so exasperated by her constant anxious questioning, and yet I could not pull back for I had allowed myself to

love her in a way that contradicted reality, our two persons, my own needs.

Sometimes I was foolishly innocent and vulnerable, trusting in a kindness I was used to in lovers. After one performance I was in the kitchen, preparing a midnight supper. Happy to be there in my house with her, happily singing to myself, "Wouldn't it be loverly" as I stirred the soup, ". . .lots of chocolates for me to eat, lots of coals making lots of heat"—wallowing in intimations of domestic comfort with her, someday, to live together, eat together every day—"warm heart, warm hands, warm feet, now wouldn't it be loverly. . . ." Excruciating to remember how I was—silly warbling fool, singing the verses over and over—when suddenly her voice cut across mine with blunt cruelty.

"I hate that song!"

Instant heaviness in my chest. Tears suddenly at my eyelids, as if she had struck me across the face.

It was an hour later, after a tense dinner and a labored discussion, started by me, about my feeling hurt, and the dynamics of her family situation that may have made her act that way—it was only after this circuitous discussion that her true motivation came out. Revenge. Revenge for a criticism I had made of the performance! I was amazed, and began to feel hopeless. There we were in the middle of the night, I at least exhausted and wishing I were soundly asleep, she hurt and I hurt, and neither of us knowing how to make it right.

I believe it was when she started to work with a therapist on the problems with her father that her rage began to boil out at me. Awareness of that man came strongly to her—that crazy father who had weighed so heavily on her, needy, unpredictable, miserable, frustrated, trying to be kind, then turning brutal, harassing Ahnie, criticizing her: this man had made a hell of her childhood. I was confronted with unreasoning fury at the dinner table. Ahnie accused me of putting her down, of smothering her, of dragging on her. Ahnie's hatred was like a wall of steel between us. I did not understand what happened in therapy that aroused her cruelty and directed it at me. I could not accept the rightness of that: it seemed hideously unfair, and I fought back, my fury rising to cover my hurt, until we wounded each other equally.

As the summer settled to its still, hot, slumbering core, she withdrew into this struggle with the memory of her father, and asked me to be patient until she resolved it. But at moments when I was least protected, the rage spewed out on me like molten lead. One morning I got up from Ahnie's bed after a terrible night. "Do you want me to drive you home?" she asked sleepily. "No." She turned over, settled in to go back to sleep, mumbled, "I'll call you later." I went out into the morning. It was seven a.m. on a Sunday. As I started up the broken sidewalk toward High Street, grief took me. Tears streamed down my cheeks. I made the long walk to the bus choking and sobbing, not bothering to hide my distress from the few joggers who came bouncing past. I felt strung out and crazy the rest of the day, lifted out of my life, floating in dangerous space, my head buzzing, my stomach tight with anxiety. The tears kept coming.

Next morning I sat for a long time on my back porch, looking at the grass that needed cutting, watching a fat robin pick about under the old tree. Again and again I saw the picture of myself leaving Ahnie's apartment, and wondered how I, Rose Giannini, who had always been so cautious, could have allowed myself to get into that condition. Surely in choosing Ahnie I had not chosen that!

As I prepared to go to work that day, however, I saw a glimmer of hope, for Ahnie was going off soon to Lake Erie, where she would stay for a month. She needed to be by herself, she said, to read, to think, to stare out over that great expanse of water. Perhaps while she was gone I could think about all this with some clarity. Maybe I could decide what to do.

During the month away, Ahnie wrote me only one letter, in which she told me about her schedule of swimming and sunbathing, how she loved the long hours of solitude. In her absence I began to see my friends again. I went to my nephew's tennis match and took my favorite niece shopping. My sisters invited me to dinner and I accepted. I felt the love of these people surrounding me, beginning to heal me. In my evenings at home alone, I pondered all the misgivings I had had since I met Ahnie, thought over our time together. A message began to make itself heard in me. Anticipating Ahnie's return, I summoned all the strength I had.

We sat across my living room from each other. She had just driven into town and wore a brown-patterned scarf tied over her shining hair. It was very unbecoming, I thought, and was glad she did not look her most appealing. As I talked, I watched her mouth tremble and open, her body huddle into itself. It was as if I were seeing that child she had been, the scrawny daughter, unloved, untended, abused by the one parent who had stayed with her. Even as I went on saying the things I needed to say, I felt a great sinking in myself, a sorrow that had nothing to do with Ahnie the adult, and that would not leave me after she was gone.

First Ahnie argued, then she screamed at me, calling me a possessive, smothering bitch. I shouted back at her, until we had said all the ugliest, most damaging things we could summon up about each other.

Ahnie perched on the arm of my couch, her body anxious, prepared for flight.

"I don't think we should see each other anymore," she said, and I was relieved she had said it, so I wouldn't have to.

"I feel the same."

We sat in excruciating silence for a time.

"No meetings, no phone calls."

"Right."

Again silence.

She got up quickly to go to the doorway, where she turned, her shoulders pulled slightly forward, to look back at me. I saw the clean lines of her face clenched tight, her eyes a cloudy, dull blue. Ahnie hesitated, as if there were something more she would say to me, and for one foolish instant I hoped she could bring forth words that might make it all right. But, still silent, she turned her back, and then she was gone.

That day I sobbed brokenly for a long time, sitting in a friend's back yard, lying across her bed. My friend wanted to comfort me, but there was no comfort for this—no one could make it better. Ahnie gone from me.

In the next weeks the moments of my life were haunted by
her. Her voice one day as we had entered my house: "I like the
smell of your house." I so pleased by that, knowing my house
smelled of fresh air and sunlight and perhaps of me. Certain moments—as one day I had brought something to her at the studio
just before she was to teach a class. She was delighted to see me,
meeting me at the door, leaning to kiss me. I looked past her into the studio where dancers were posed or lazily stretching in the
dim underwater light of the room, mysterious. I was wracked at
night by the remembrance of her body curled behind me, in this
very bed. Every room of this house I live in was a place where
we had talked together, eaten together, held each other, argued.
Old brown-shingled house with deep porch and wide eaves: it
thrust Ahnie at me. The back yard brought her to me strongly,
especially the afternoons before her performances when we had
sat in the yard and I was there to help her tolerate her nervous-
ness. I heard her voice speaking, saying, "You are very sweet,"
saying, "I love you."

Despite our promise, Ahnie called me several times, and we
talked in a sad, hurtful way to each other. After each phone call,
I went into my bedroom and cried, wanting Ahnie still.

I plunged into my work each day, shutting out for hours at a
time the impressions of her that entered between me and what I
was doing. I went out with friends, my heart bruised each time
we approached a place where I had been with Ahnie. Once again
I participated in the lives of my nieces and nephews, accepting
my role of wise generous aunt. There was time now to drink
coffee with my sisters, listen to their tales of husbands and children. But still I awoke sometimes in the middle of the night with
the longing for Ahnie strong in me.

Then finally the heat lifted and it was autumn, the air sharp
as apple cider, excitement building as the students returned to
Ohio State University, the football season began. A new year,
like all the others. I swept the yellow leaves from the sidewalk
in back of my house; in the cold twilight I built a fire and
breathed the smoke. Turning to look at my house, shabby and
old-fashioned in the near dark, I was filled with affection for it.
All the past it held for me: ourselves as children; Papa stum-

bling tiredly out the back door in his plaster-spotted overalls to sit on the steps, inhale the grass smell, rest; Mama in her last weeks, lying still and gazing out that upstairs window down into the yard. This was my place which sheltered and explained me. I was the same age Mama had been when Papa died—a middle-aged woman, settled, half of my life behind me. The autumn brought its reminders of loss; it let me understand I was larger than the events in my life, more enduring than any particular pain.

Nothing Safe in Crabtree Meadow

When I wake, it is so cold that my cheeks are numb; all around me the night is thickly black under a starless sky. The sound comes again—metal on rock. One of our cook pans is being moved at the fire pit. A marmot, I think, and lie listening. Squirrels and chipmunks aren't big enough to move a pan like that.

Silence.

Then another noise. I listen with strained attention, trying to identify it. *Either* it is the sound of my son Rob unzipping his sleeping bag, *or*—and my scalp tingles—or it is the sound of claws dragging across canvas.

Stealthily, a little at a time, I turn over on the ground inside my sleeping bag until I lie facing Rob. Now in his eighteenth year he is already broad-shouldered and sturdily muscled. His big body lies turned away from me. Fast asleep.

There is another scratching noise, loud in the night.

I turn over again, slowly, as quietly as possible, and when I am lying on my right side I unzip the top of my mummy bag and reach a careful hand out into the cold to close it around the flashlight. I direct it at our packs, propped against the log near our feet, and flick the switch.

Looking straight at me in the circle of light are two yellow eyes in a dark furry head. The animal is hunched over from behind the log, his massive forelegs wrapped around my pack.

The light does not frighten him. He goes on ripping at the side pocket of the pack, pulling things out the hole he's made.

My body is paralyzed for a few moments, while my mind leaps back to a conversation with some campers in Junction Meadow. "Make noise," they had advised, "yell. Jump up and down. Beat on pans. Only don't mess with a female bear who has cubs." How can I know the sex of this beast who is pulling a tube of peanut butter from the pocket of the pack, staring me in the eyes all the while?

I desperately want this not to be happening. Oh how I wish this were not happening.

Keeping the flashlight on him, I sit up, unzipping my bag farther, and I start to yell—a karate yell, from the diaphragm, deafening, terrifying. But all that comes out of my tight throat is Eeeeeeeeep, eeeeeeeep, eeeeeeeep.

The creature goes on looting my pack. I keep moving backwards as I try to yell, until I'm practically sitting on top of Rob in his sleeping bag. He grumbles and rolls away.

Yellow claws pull a chocolate bar from the frayed hole in the canvas. The small shiny eyes watch me, the enormous furry shoulders hunch tighter around the pack.

I struggle upright out of my warm covering and dance in my thermal underwear on top of my sleeping bag, shouting Hup, hup, hup!

What the hell's wrong with my hardy teenage son? Why doesn't he get up to help me?

I leap and stamp and throw one arm out like a pump handle, my yell getting louder now.

The little eyes watch me warily as the claws pull a bag of trail food from the hole and stuff it in the mouth, spilling peanuts

and sunflower seeds down the front of the pack as the plastic
splits.

I jump in the cold air, knees jerking up and down, shouting
Yow, yow, yow! I'm afraid to turn away from the bear to find
out what Rob is doing.

Out comes a tampax. The animal shoves it in his mouth, bites
into it, and one half is left dangling like a cigar butt down his
chin.

God *damn* it! Here I am, dancing like a madwoman and
screeching not eight feet from him and he just goes on with his
midnight snack. "Throw something," they had said in Junction
Meadow.

All I have is the flashlight. I pull back my arm, aim, let fly.

It sails toward him and bounces off his head just above his
eyes, spiralling up, its beam of light looping crazily in the darkness.

The bear stops all motion, stunned. And in that instant I
know I have made a terrible mistake, for something was illumi-
nated by the spinning flashlight beam, something small and furry
moving up behind the log. I just glimpsed it. Now I look around
for a place to run to. The bear's great body rears up clumsily off
the pack, hesitates, and I get ready to go. Anywhere! Up the
nearest tree—no. She can scramble up after me. Out through
the underbrush in the dark—but surely she can move in it faster
than I. The creek is too far down the slope. There *is* no place
to go.

The moment seems endless as she teeters there on her hind
legs, her cub shuffling about in the weeds behind her. I understand fully what I've done, now. The knowledge paralyzes me.

And then with astonishing speed she has scrambled over the
log and comes thrashing toward me. I turn to run just as she
lunges forward on her hind legs. The raging weight of her drags
me down, claws tear at my back. I scream and struggle against
thick rough fur. She mauls me in the dirt, holds me in a crush-
ing murderous embrace, as the pain rips down my side from my
shoulder. Her rank odor curls my nostrils. I see the black sky
above her black head, my mind filled with her roaring.

* * *

It has been a quiet morning. Earlier the garbage men
thumped their way through the basement and out again as their
truck grumbled in the street. But I was already awake. I don't
sleep as I did before, all night long.

Rob brought me some tea and toast. He stroked my face.
He knelt before me and asked me how I am, does my shoulder
hurt? Can he do anything to make me more comfortable? His
dark red curls fall down over his forehead, his eyes are a mottled
greenish brown in his sunburned face. I smile at him, wishing
he were not so anxious.

On our first night here at home, I asked him to explain. Pa-
tiently he told me each of the thoughts that passed through his
mind as he lay there almost asleep, each one giving him an excuse not to act or confusing him, until the final moment when
he saw the light wobble crazily in the darkness and thought it
was a space ship landing, or someone with a flashlight stumbling
down upon us. He is good-natured and big for his eighteen
years; he has enormous feet, thick wrists, and a weird science
fiction-filled imagination. My beloved son. Perhaps there
would have been nothing he could have done that night. My
anger at him passed quickly. Still, he says he feels guilty, and I
can see in the tentative way he looks at me that he suffers.

He brings me books and magazines; he describes the movies
I could watch on TV. Today there will be *Flying Down to Rio*
with Fred Astaire and Ginger Rogers, or maybe I'd like to flip
the channel to. . . a star-filled afternoon. How about it, mom?

It seemed we were caught in a dream as Rob cut away the
shreds of my thermal underwear top and bound a T-shirt around
my shoulder. Dawn light was arriving. Trees, branches began to
appear out of the darkness. I sat propped against the log. I remember how heavy my head felt, hanging down, as I stared at
the blood spreading on the white cotton of the T-shirt bandage.

Then there was the ordeal of getting my trousers on, and my
boots, for I would not let Rob go off by himself to get help. I
would not be left alone in Crabtree Meadow, wounded and vulnerable. There was a ranger station just at the other end of the
meadow; it was there Rob would take me. He got a belt, put
it around my neck and rested my arm in it like a sling. Then he

wrapped a jacket around my shoulders and lifted me to my feet. I tottered sideways, grabbing at him with my good arm, as the pain engulfed me in a dizzying wave. He wanted to carry me. But I told him I would walk. Just to feel the ground under my feet, to move one leg forward, then the other, kept me connected to consciousness.

When we got to the ranger station, we found it locked and deserted. I remember the padlock hanging on the door, with its little key-shaped mouth.

I sat on the stoop, and it was then I noticed that my whole side from shoulder to knee had turned scarlet. I'm finished, I thought, all my body fluids are leaving me, I'll be dry inside soon, white and weightless. My brain will stop. My heart will go slower and slower until there is no more blood to pump.

A ragged whimpering sound came to me. I looked up to where Rob leaned against the door of the hut, bent forward and shaking. Tears ran down over his dirty hands, making pale crooked tracks in the dust on his skin.

* * *

The magazines are piled on the floor next to my chair. I'm not interested in reading. If they'd let me, I'd go back to my job tomorrow. But instead I must stay in this room and receive the guilty ministrations of Rob and the visits of Mrs. Linenthal who comes down from 2B to see me. I'm not even sure Mrs. Linenthal likes me; certainly I've never fulfilled her expectations for someone my age. I am a small woman, and even now in my fifties I am feisty and quick. I don't mean that I seem younger than my age. No, older even, if you look at my face. But I am the person I've become.

Rob says, "I think mom's tired now. She wants to rest." And he leads Mrs. Linenthal out of my room, leaving me alone again.

I know I'm difficult for them to understand. They expect me to need their comfort. But, as I said, I am the person I've become in all these years of living, and what engages me now is the mystery of my actions that night. How, when it seemed I would surely be killed, was I able to get my right arm free, bring up my fist, and hit blindly at the one sensitive and unprotected spot on the animal's body, the nose. And hurt or startled, she staggered away from me and ran into the underbrush, her cub waddling after her.

* * *

The campers who arrived in Crabtree Meadow that morning were two young men and a woman, all about Rob's age. They were carrying enormous packs, and they had tanned legs under loose hiking shorts. While the two men worked with Rob to cut poles and drape a poncho over them to make a stretcher, the woman knelt before me. "Let me give you some water," she said. And she unscrewed the canteen for me and was going to hold it to my mouth until I took it from her with my good hand. When I tilted my head back to drink, I saw a blue jay sitting on a low limb of a tree. The jay cocked its head, regarded me for a few moments, and then began to squawk. I stared helplessly up at it while it screeched insults at me, chiding and complaining. And I thought, I'm done for.

They loaded me carefully on the stretcher, and while one young man ran off to try to locate the ranger, the woman and Rob and the other man carried me out of the meadow on the trail going west. I shut my eyes against the sky's brightness. My body rolled in the poncho, limbs jiggling, until I felt the nausea pressing up out of my stomach. The men's and the woman's voices came—short utterances as they struggled to keep me level on a steep incline, as they waded through a stream. "Careful now." "Protect her shoulder." "Watch out!" Their grunts and strenuous breathing surrounded me.

My stomach roiled as I breathed the stink of bear musk clinging to my skin.

* * *

Rob and I were hiking through Sequoia National Forest toward Mt. Whitney in hot dry August.

That evening we had made it to Crabtree Meadow, where we were the only people. The sun was behind the mountain, and a swatch of apricot-colored cloud hung above the ridge in a clear blue sky. All was silent, except for the rush of Whitney Creek below us.

After eating, we propped our packs against a log, spread out the sleeping bags, not bothering with a tent. Normally we would have hung our food supplies high up on a tree limb, but in our eight days of hiking we had seen no sign of bear, and this night we let fatigue overcome our better judgment.

Exhausted and peaceful, we lay in our warm sleeping bags and talked about the last few days, which had been tough ones.

Two nights before, only eighteen miles from Whitney, we had been stopped by a forest fire across the Wallace Creek Trail. Closing my eyes I could see it, burning quietly in the windless night, eating away at the trees and underbrush on the ridge above Junction Meadow where we had been camped. Orange flames crawled the tree trunks, bushes ignited, sizzled, flared up, branches fell, spraying sparks. It burned with a curious sound like paper crumpling.

To get around the fire, we had to go eight miles out of our way up the Tyndall Creek Trail. That day we came up 2,800 feet in eight miles, on short switchbacks up a steep mountainside, with no shade. It was the hardest climb we'd done.

But hiking the next day was glorious. The trees on the slopes up to Bighorn Plateau were yellow pines or sugar pines—dead but still standing, without bark, in twisted spiralled shapes, their wood the color of poured honey.

And then the plateau itself, where we had experienced that great lift to the spirits, the elation of the high country. Eleven thousand feet high and perfectly bare, Bighorn Plateau offered a view of almost 360 degrees. We took off our packs and walked across the wide dome to its center. Furry orange marmots came out of their holes to peer at us, sneak up to examine our packs. We sat on the rocks taking swigs of warmish water from the canteen, looking around us to blue distant peaks. West to the ranges we had come from, north toward Forrester's Pass, and southeast in the direction of Mt. Whitney.

It was delicious to let these pictures move through my mind, as I lay in my mummy bag, the muscles of my legs slowly relaxing, the sound of the creek lulling me. We were safe in Crabtree Meadow, and until morning there was nothing that had to be done.

"I think we'll make it up Mt. Whitney tomorrow, after all," came Rob's drowsy voice from his sleeping bag.

Those words were like a float bobbing on the surface of an ocean into which I sank, farther and farther down, until they with everything else had disappeared and I lay in exhausted, dreamless sleep.

When I woke, it was so cold that my cheeks were numb; all around me the night was thickly black under a starless sky. The sound came again—metal on rock. One of our cook pans was being moved at the fire pit.

And I lay still and thought, this is a dream, the dream is always like this.

Another noise. I listened with strained attention, trying to identify it. Either it was the sound of Rob unzipping his sleeping bag, or—and my scalp tingled—or it was the sound of claws dragging across canvas.

The dream is always like this, right up to that denser bulk of darkness lumbering toward me, engulfing me, pulling me down farther into chaos than I can stand to go, the ground made wet beneath me, my mind falling out the back of my head. Rob cannot enter between us now as I wonder if in the muscles of that animal there is the memory of my body caught against it, whether my odor lingers in her nostrils or has made its trace in her brain. Did she, cleaning herself the next day, lick my blood from between her claws along with the twigs and moss and dried pine needles lodged there?

I wake, my injured back throbbing, to stare up into the darkness of my room, wait for morning light, for the day's requirements to assemble me once again out of the night's vast disorder into my familiar, finite self.

The
Cutting Room

A glistening, rose-colored pear balances on the marble block.
Dr. Barakian holds it firmly, lifts the knife, cuts through.
  "The uterus is opened laterally to reveal. . ."
  He picks up a tiny metal ruler and places it against the cut
surface.
  ". . .to reveal a velvety 2 millimeter endometrial surface."
  As the doctor speaks into the dictaphone above the laboratory table where he works, Kelly, who stands near him, goes on
separating number tags and placing them on the tops of the
plastic containers arranged in a row before her. In the jars are
suspended shreds of red tissue from D & C's, little nubbins of
warts, delicate milky cataracts floating like anemone, the yellowish pinkish bag of a gall bladder with its stones lying on the bottom of the jar.
  The dictaphone belt turns as Dr. Barakian cuts and talks. He
dumps the fragments of the uterus back in the jar of formalin
and reaches for the ovary.

46

". . .consists of two small fragments of white fibrous tissue grossly consistent with ovarian stroma. . . ."

Kelly thinks how her daughter would appreciate those words. On hearing them, Kim would envision a space taxi streaking toward the ovarian stroma in the far depths of the universe. It is only by resorting to such fantasies that Kelly is able to maintain her sense of humor in the cutting room.

She goes out the swinging door and down the hall to the transcription room, where her two sister-workers are attached to their dictaphones, typewriters clacking away. As the newest person she has been given the task of receiving the specimens when they are brought up from surgery each morning and afternoon, assigning them numbers, writing the pertinent identifying details in a large black book, and taking the specimens into the cutting room where the pathologist cuts them open and describes them. When he hired her, Dr. Rook had explained, "Everything that is taken out in surgery comes up here to us. We do a gross report—that is, what can be seen with the naked eye—and then samples of the tissue are made into microscope slides by the cytologist, and we look at them and do a microscopic report."

Kelly reaches for one of the tapes on the desk near her and slaps it into her dictaphone. She attaches the earpiece, then stops to light a cigarette.

Across from her, Brenda begins to mutter furiously.

Kelly glances up to watch Brenda open the top of the yellow pathology report form, unscrew her little bottle of liquid paper, and begin correcting the mistake on each of the five carbons. The thick waves of auburn hair bob on Brenda's head as she gives the bottle a vicious shake and pulls out the brush to jab at the paper. Her motions are speeded up by the coffee and cigarettes she uses just to stay awake for her ambitious schedule, in which, besides this job, she moonlights at another hospital on weekends and attends night classes at State College.

Kelly experiences periodic mild amazement at Brenda's lifestyle. A placid person herself, who enjoys moving slowly, she keeps up with Brenda in only one area—the consuming of cigarettes. By 9:30 a.m. the two of them have filled the small windowless room with clouds of grey smoke.

"Gross Report," Kelly types, and adds to herself, "I'll say!"

"Goddammit, I want a raise!" It is Brenda's voice, grumbling away as she dabs on the liquid paper. "It takes everything I fucking know to do this job, and I know plenty. I'm overqualified for this joint. If I was a *man,* you know I'd be *managing* this place and pulling down a decent salary."

Her angry eyes look up to meet Kelly's and Kelly answers, "That's right, you *should* be the boss. You're just the type to push people around."

Brenda blinks, and then grins slowly, and finally breaks up into loose laughter.

"Fuck it anyway," she adds.

At the third side of the triangular white desk, Josie sits with lowered eyes. She is younger than the other women, one of many daughters in a large Filipino-American family. Her breasts are pushed up by a tortuous bra inside her tight clothes. She is anxious to be voluptuous for her husband, a handsome student who likes to tell her how the young women at the college pursue him.

It was probably Josie who started it, but Kelly didn't hear the first part because the orderly had just brought her two small unmarked containers of D & C, and had given her the two slips that went with them. She was occupied in looking at these when she heard Josie's voice talking softly across the desk to Brenda.

"You know that Gerald, that black guy that's a lab tech and always wears those beautiful clothes? Yesterday, Bill from surgery told me he's a *faggot!* Can you *believe* it?!"

There comes a slight catch in Kelly's breathing, just a little pause between breaths. She glances up to see Brenda squinting disdainfully at Josie through a cloud of smoke.

"Well, you *can't always tell,* you know," Brenda instructs Josie.

Kelly shuffles the lab slips, moves the containers of reddish liquid.

"I mean, how about Betty in the lab?" Brenda adds.

"Which Betty?"

"You know. Sometimes she comes in here to ask about the autopsies."

"You mean that really cute girl?"

"Yeah."

"Well, what *about* her?"

"She's one."

"No!" Josie's smooth face puckers.

Kelly's stomach begins to shake as if the nerves jangling on the surface of her body sent tremors in to a point under her belly button.

"Yeah, she's a lesbian," Brenda continues. "She's lovers with Donna. They *live* together."

"But she has *long hair!*" A squeal of dismay from Josie.

If either of the other women were to look at Kelly, she thinks, they would surely see her discomfort. But they are absorbed in their conversation.

Lighting a cigarette, pulling in the harsh smoke, she asks herself, Should I tell them? A part of her answers, Yes, just say it and put a stop to this. Another part of her argues, What business is it of theirs? Why should I explain myself to them?

When she looked in the mirror this morning she saw a round-faced woman with blond smooth medium-length hair, large earnest brown eyes. That was definitely a lesbian looking back at her from the mirror. But apparently when Brenda and Annie look at her they see a heterosexual woman like themselves, or they would not be talking this way in her presence.

"That Donna is one, no mistake," Josie says. "I mean, she's so *mannish*."

Kelly strains every nerve to pay attention to the lab slips on the desk. She stubs out her cigarette and reaches for the big black log book to write in the information. When she has transcribed the women's names, surgical numbers, and surgical procedure in the book, she looks up at the two containers. There they sit, next to each other, identical, and without markings.

Panic comes thumping up in her. My god, I don't know which is which!

Brenda and Josie have gone back to typing, the clatter of their machines loud in the room. Kelly sits beneath this noise, her face burning, and stares with stricken eyes at the two jars. In paying so much attention to that conversation, in getting up-

set about it, she had forgotten to keep the slips with the respect-
ive bottles, a rule strictly followed to avoid mix-up. Now she
has the two slips, one for Mrs. Romerio, one for Mrs. Sanchez,
and there sit the two bottles with their pinkish shreds floating
in clear liquid. Kelly knows that both Mrs. Sanchez and Mrs.
Romerio went to their gynecologists, lay on the table with their
knees up, allowed the doctor to put his hand in their vaginas,
open their cervices and insert a knife; allowed him to scrape the
linings of their uterii and put the scrapings in these two bottles.
The pathologist looking through his or her microscope will discover the condition of the cells, and the doctor will know how
to proceed. Hysterectomy? Removal of the cervix? With these
thoughts Kelly rejects the temptation to cover her mistake by
simply putting one lab slip with each jar and sending it on. She
sits holding the jars, feeling ill.

Finally Brenda looks up from her work to take a drag of her
cigarette.

"What's the *matter,* Kelly?" she asks in alarm.

Kelly swallows, and hears her voice tremble slightly as she
talks. "Brenda, help me. I don't know which of these D & C's
goes with which slip."

"Oh." A short, flat sound like breath being knocked out.
Brenda stares into Kelly's eyes for a moment, then down at the
glass jars, then up again. Her mouth stays part way open.

"Is there any way I can find out which is which before I have
to take them to Dr. Rook?"

Josie is listening now, too. Both she and Brenda look as if
they are witnessing an auto accident.

"I don't know. . .how you would. . ." Brenda begins.

"Ask one of the other pathologists," Josie suggests.

Brenda brightens. "Yeah, ask Dr. Wong!"

When they have a problem, they go to the one woman pathologist. It is always easier to talk to Dr. Wong because she pays
attention to what they say and then she talks with them about
what can be done. The male pathologists treat them like children, or seem strangely embarrassed by their presence, or sit staring at their legs while they talk.

Walking down the hall to Dr. Wong's office, Kelly struggles with the emotions dislodged and running rampant in her like a river in flood.

"All is not lost," Dr. Wong says when Kelly has finished talking. "The specimens can be distinguished from each other when the tissue is looked at through a microscope."

Kelly breathes a little more easily.

"But you'll have to take them in to Dr. Rook and explain what's happened so that when the slides arrive he'll be able to recognize them."

Dr. Wong's broad gentle face creases in sympathy. Everyone in the lab is afraid of Dr. Rook; even the other pathologists stay our of his way.

"I'm sorry, but it's *his* day to do the micros. You'll have to let him know."

It was just this encounter that Kelly wanted to avoid. Leaving Dr. Wong's office, she walks very slowly up the corridor. Rook is the head pathologist, a brilliant and imperious man who flies into a rage if everything is not done exactly as he wishes.

The paper of the surgery slips has begun to wrinkle in Kelly's sweaty grip. She holds tightly to the jars. Dropping them now would be the final disaster. Against all her instincts, she forces herself to approach Dr. Rook's door. When she arrives there, she carefully shifts papers and jars to one hand, takes a deep breath, and knocks. Not loud.

"Come in," says a sharp male voice.

* * *

Kelly's afternoon is nightmarish. Her mind spins wildly as she works to maintain her composure and do her job. I don't know how to manage this, she thinks, looking across the white desk at Brenda and Josie, who seem now to be separated from her by a chasm. In all her previous jobs—at the Buick dealership, at the insurance office, in the other hospitals where she worked—in all those offices she had been a married lady. A nice heterosexual woman with a child. There was nothing to explain, nothing to reveal. But in the year since she left her last job she has become a lesbian, and that choice has magically transported her into another state of mind. She was so extremely uncomfortable as they talked of faggots and lesbians this morning. She wanted to explain.

Now she stares across at Josie's young face. I know something about her life, she thinks. I know what it's like to work to put your husband through school. I know what it's like to live for a man, caring for him, seeing no future for yourself separate from him. I know something of Josie's life. But what would Josie think of *me* if she knew? Kelly had been straight long enough to know the opinions most heterosexuals hold about homosexuals. She herself had considered "queers" to be sick, sad, partial or undeveloped people; until she became one and found that she was still herself, stronger and more sure of who she was, loving a woman.

Bill from surgery arrives with the tray of specimens.

"How's your love life?" he asks, grinning at each of the three women as he sets the tray of containers before Kelly.

"Better than yours, I'd be willin' to bet!" snaps Brenda.

"Well now. . ." Bill straightens up, inflates his chest. "Maybe you'd like to find out for yourself. . . ."

Kelly lifts the jars off the tray and begins checking them against the surgery slips, ignoring Bill.

A laugh of exaggerated scorn comes from Brenda.

Hearing Josie's giggle, Kelly glances up to see a red flush appear on Bill's bull neck. His eyes are locked on Brenda's face as she goes on typing, and Kelly sees in them a look of dull hatred. But he shifts his weight, rolls his eyes, and gestures with his thumb at Brenda.

"Get *her*!" he says, and mumbles, "Who'd want it anyway?" as he shoulders his way out the door, walking tough.

Now that his urgent pay-attention-to-*me* energy is gone, Kelly concentrates on the jars. At first it had been difficult to accept the specimens. Especially the first mastectomy. But she forced herself to take the top off the jar and look. The liquid formalin was pinkish with blood. The breast floated nipple down. She saw the spongy whitish tissue of the inside, clumped together like massed blossoms; she saw the severed skin. Looking into the jar, Kelly thought of the woman in the bed on some other floor of the hospital. She felt as if it were herself. Trembling, she put the lid on the jar and sat looking nowhere. She had read about unnecessary surgery on women, the doctors who make fortunes removing uterii and ovaries and breasts. Was this horror one of those operations just for the doctor's gain? Finally she picked up the surgery slip to read the diagnosis. Carcinogenic tumor. She was reassured. She decided to believe that this was necessary. They removed it so the woman can go on living, she told herself. Awful as it is, you can live and walk and do everything without a breast.

During the first few days on the job, Kelly had existed in a state of seminausea and shock. Here in the pathology department it was impossible to avoid the knowledge that human beings are flesh. Chunks of meat can be cut from them and put in a jar, quickly turning greyish in the formaldehyde solution. Pickled meat. Kelly had worked in hospitals before, but she had worked with living, complaining patients. Here in the pathology department, the only intact human beings who arrived for the doctors' attentions were corpses. Everything else had been dismantled. For days Kelly would suffer visual flashes of the specimens while she was eating dinner, would dream that she was dissecting a body in a basement room, sweating in panic because she didn't know how.

Now she looks at the large jar before her on the desk, inside which a being is curled. One tiny hand rests against the wall of the jar; the hand is almost transparent, with perfect little fingers slightly flexed.

The lab slip tells Kelly that the young woman came bleeding to the emergency room. Hemorrhage—what a dark, swollen word it is. Kelly looks at the fetus, so still and somehow peaceful in its bath of formalin.

"Jesus, that Bill is a jerk!" Brenda comments. "Can you imagine what his wife had to put up with before she divorced him?"

Kelly places the specimens on the tray and carries them out of the transcription room down the hall and through the swinging doors into the laboratory. Long black tables with sinks in

them cross the room. In the air hangs the sweetish smell of
formalin.

Through a window is the morgue. Kelly sees Dr. Rook at
work, his small neat head thrust forward over the corpse, the
lenses of his glasses glittering in the bright light. The body is an
old man, his skin yellowish, his genitals lying sideways on his
stringy thigh. Dr. Rook is lifting out the internal organs from
the gaping red chest cavity, and once again Kelly is surprised at
the bright colors, the yellow fat, the blue veins, the purplish or
scarlet or pink tissue of the organs.

But she hurries past the window, hoping Dr. Rook will not
see her. The visit to his office had been so embarrassing that she
wishes she might never see him again. It had been extremely difficult to open his door and step inside, clutching her slips of paper, her two little jars. It had felt like the end of the world.
And then to find there were three other doctors crammed into
the small office with Dr. Rook. Everyone stopped talking. They
stared at her as if she were one of the specimens. "I've made a
mistake, Dr. Rook." (How hard it was to say those words under
the eyes of the four men.) "I don't know which slip goes with
which jar. Dr. Wong said you. . ."

Rook's eyebrows shot up.

"*That,*" he bellowed, "is not *allowed!*"

One of the men smiled.

Kelly stared into Rook's bright challenging eyes. She waited
a few moments. "Dr. Wong said you could tell the difference
under the microscope. . ."

Rook stared at her. "She did, did she?"

Again Kelly waited, confused. The one thing she hadn't expected was to be played with.

"Yes. She said if I let you know now, when it came to the
micro report you could tell them apart."

"Yes, yes." Now he was impatient. "Give them here."

He snatched the bottles and papers from her and dropped
them on a desk piled high with books and magazines and lab
reports.

Kelly turned to go quickly out the door. She hurried down
the hall to the coffee room, which was deserted at that hour,

and stood inside the door biting hard on the knuckles of her
fist to stop the trembling and the need to cry.

* * *

Brenda is putting on her coat with its thick imitation fur collar, snapping shut her purse.

"I've got exactly 18 minutes to get out to State for my special
studies seminar," she grumbles to Kelly.

Josie waves to Kelly from the doorway. "Take care. See you
tomorrow."

When they are gone, Kelly sees that Brenda has left her last
cigarette burning in the ashtray. The smoke drifts up, silent
and serene.

How wrong it feels to find herself so alienated from Brenda
and Josie now. The three of them in this little room have developed a loyalty; they stick together, defend each other against
the doctors when they can, help each other out when one of
them gets behind. She felt accepted by them from her first day
on the job.

Kelly rips a report from her typewriter and begins reading it
over.

For Brenda and Josie, nothing has changed, she thinks. Somehow the madness of this whole thing is that only *I* know that
anything has happened. They didn't notice any reaction from
me when they were talking. Probably they'd never catch on if
I were to pretend, if I just laughed at the jokes, went along with
the speculation on who is queer and who isn't. But she knows
how alone she has felt during this whole long dreadful day, how
filled with a discomfort that had some of the sticky quality of
shame. That alarmed her, for it reminded her of the many contradictory feelings she had experienced during the period in
which she recognized her love for women and began to act on it.
Delight would give way suddenly to terror. Will everyone hate
me now that I'm queer? she would wonder, and her own hatred
of self would come crashing in. Then she would feel strong
again, in possession of herself, launched on a new life. A day
later she would be tentative and frightened, ready to flee back

into the supposed safety of heterosexuality. It had taken many months, and the help of a number of lesbian women besides her lover, for her to be secure in her new identity.

Now here I am, she thinks, having to go through this again! Her desire is desperate—to escape the building, to break free and walk, mulling over today's incident in her mind, away from the scene. Perhaps she will see it differently. Is it way out of proportion?

She peers at the report form in her hands, reading, "There is no nuclear dyskaryosis and no demonstrable mitotic activity in these areas. . . ."

How drained and frayed she feels. And crazy. Yes, absolutely nuts.

Dr. Barakian, large in his rumpled suit, comes through the door and drops a stack of dictaphone tapes on the desk. He blinks at her from behind thick glasses. "These can wait till tomorrow."

Kelly nods, watching him turn to leave.

Ten minutes to go. As the newest transcriptionist, she has to stay until 5:30, but usually she is glad for this last hour of relative quiet. Today each minute of it is torture. Brenda's and Josie's conversation keeps replaying in her head. Kelly lights a cigarette, one of too many she has smoked today, and draws the bitter smoke into her stale-tasting mouth. Exhaling, she wonders, at which point could she have said something? Said *what*? What could she have done differently so that the mistake with the D & C's wouldn't have happened?

She spreads her arms on the desk, staring up at the clock. I never want to live through another day like this, she knows, and there comes the realization that there is an endless succession of such days ahead of her, of situations in which she will suffer this anxious interior drama. Already she has experienced it, for in the preceding weeks she had often thought of telling Brenda and Josie about her life. They talked of husband and boyfriend, and she talked about her daughter and her "roommate," not able to say "my lover" or speak of the commitment and the passion of that bond. She had felt like a liar.

Mechanically, she puffs on her cigarette, watching the smoke coil out into the room, and she knows her decision is made. Yet for a moment she remembers stories told her, of harassment and deliberate cruelty, of jobs lost because some person in authority could not bear the presence of a "queer." Kelly tightens her jaw, pushing away this information. Tomorrow I'm going to eat lunch with Brenda in the cafeteria, she thinks, and I'm going to tell her I'm a lesbian. She imagines Brenda's response: she'll probably pretend she knows all about lesbians. Maybe she took a course on us out at State. Kelly does not like the bitterness of that thought. She attempts to continue quite practically. The next day I'll ask Josie to go to lunch with me and I'll tell *her* I'm a lesbian. That will be harder, because she'll probably feel guilty for all the remarks she's made about faggots. And her curiosity about lesbian sex might get aroused. Oh, I hope not. And anyone else they may tell can react however they will!

Easily said, but she does not like to imagine what Bill may do with the information. Or the doctors, if it should get to them.

With deliberate slowness, Kelly puts aside the finished report and unfolds the typewriter cover to put on her machine. She sits holding it, forgetting her purpose, as a phrase repeats in her mind. The specimen is opened to reveal. . . (Why should I have to? she objects in anger.) . . .is opened to reveal. . . .

But today's experience has been like suffocating.

Shaking herself, she pulls the cover down roughly over the typewriter and gets up to put on her coat. In the little mirror that Brenda has hung on the wall behind her desk, Kelly sees limp blond hair, round face, the expression not so different from this morning except that the eyes look out surprised and chastened. This is definitely a lesbian looking back at her from the glass.

She shuts the door on the room with its three-sided desk, its typewriters and dictaphones, and goes past the cutting room to the elevator that will take her down to the street, to what feels like freedom for the night, until the morning brings her back here for whatever will transpire.

The Day My Father Kicked Me Out

It's Sunday evening. We're sitting at the table in my parents' house in Columbus, Ohio, and I've brought a friend with me. I've invited my friend Nyla to dinner, honestly, as protection. It's been eight years since I've come out from San Francisco to visit my parents, and I'm having difficulty being here.

So anyway, we're sitting at Sunday evening dinner, which is tuna salad, as always, and my father begins his lecture on John Dillinger and Pretty Boy Floyd. This discourse is really about law and order, with these two renowned bank robbers of the thirties as villains. He rambles on about their exploits, and then he asks Nyla, Do you know what they did to Dillinger and Floyd when they caught up with them?

Nyla: What?

My father: They shot them.

My father is a big man, and he leans in on you physically when he talks to you. You can feel him pushing on you. Now he leans in on Nyla and says, And do you know what I would do *these days* with people who break the law?

Nyla has just gotten out of the hospital, where she had surgery: she's a bit weak and not quite in control. I notice when he asks her that question she starts to twitch a little, her face begins to tremble and the corners of her mouth jerk. And I remember that when Nyla and I had lived in a women's liberation collective in San Francisco, I had received a barrage of letters from my father, and the lecture on John Dillinger and Pretty Boy Floyd had been in those letters, word for word as he is giving it right now. So Nyla is having a bit of a hard time here, and my father repeats the question.

Do you know what I would do with the people who break the law *these days?*

She: I think I do.

He: What?

She: You'd shoot them.

That's right, he says.

And she goes over the edge in a cascade of giggles.

I'm appalled. This is surrealistic, for as soon as Nyla begins to laugh, I lose control too. We giggle and snort like ninnies, and neither of us can stop.

Caught in these convulsions, I realize how trying these three days with my father have been. When he wasn't criticizing me for the way I live, he has been lecturing me about Richard Nixon's innocence and how the press always persecuted that unfortunate man. He's obsessed with Nixon, and set on convincing me of his views, and he has pushed me out to teeter on the edge of hysteria.

Nyla tilts me right over.

My mother's action at this historic juncture is to get up from the table and go out on the front porch to sit on the swing.

My father tries to go on with his talk, but pretty soon it's obvious that we're laughing at him, even though we pretend we're choking and we hold our napkins over our mouths. As soon as

Nyla gets herself in control, I start again, and then when I stop, she starts.

So my father gets mad. He stands up, bangs against the table, knocks his chair over on its back, and calls us some names. (It's a funny thing, I can't remember the words he used. He may have said weirdos, and I wonder if he said queers: at that point in time he wasn't sure about me.) Finally, he goes stomping out to the porch, and he sits down next to my mother and starts to swing back and forth.

We're left in the dining room, Nyla and me, and we cannot yet stop laughing. We're helpless, the tears are running down our faces. It feels so good, it feels wonderful, yet we *know* what we've done.

We can hear the swing out on the front porch. *Scree, scree.* They're not talking, but the swing is squeaking.

At last we are calm, only an occasional giggle buzzing like a crazy hummingbird through our now-earnest talk. How are we to get Nyla out of the house?! I mean, they're on the front porch: she has to get past them somehow. Sneaking out the back door would be too cowardly. We sit here. We don't know what to do. And Nyla has developed hiccups.

Finally I agree to go with her to the front porch. We stand up and check out our faces for telltale signs of mirth; Nyla hiccups, claps her hand over her mouth, and holds her breath, bugging her eyes at me. With a long look at each other, we start for the door.

On the front porch, my parents swing back and forth—*scree, scree*—and my father stares into space as if we do not exist.

Thank you very much, hic, for having me to dinner, Nyla says.

My mother replies, You're quite welcome. We enjoyed having you.

Nyla walks down the porch steps, gets in her car, says good-bye to me with a sneaky little wave, and drives off.

Here I am, left. I go back in the house, clear the table, start washing the dishes, and I think, Well, now, what am *I* going to do about this? The longer I stay in here washing the dishes, the harder it's going to be to go out on the porch. Finally, I decide that I must go out right now to say *something*. Through the

dining room and living room I go, and step out on the porch.
My father swings back and forth, back and forth, staring straight
ahead. *Scree, scree.*

I'm sorry we laughed at you. (This is the truth, I *am* sorry.)

And he starts in, You bring your weird friends here and you
laugh at a man in his own house, and etcetera on and on, very
loudly, and he makes me mad.

Ever since I *arrived* you been laughing at *me!* I yell. Everything I do you put me down you don't like what I do, you laugh
at me, it's about time somebody laughed at *you!*

And my mother says, Please, we *do* have neighbors.

Well, the argument goes back and forth between me and my
father, because I feel outraged, and *he* feels outraged. And finally he says to me, if somebody laughs at me in my own house,
I'm gonna kick their ass out the door, and yours too!

I see my chance. Does that mean you'd like me to leave?
I ask.

Now that really puts him up against the wall. What can he
say?

Yes, it does!

I get up from my chair and I spit out, Well, it's a relief!

I go in and slam the screen door and stamp upstairs to pack
my bag.

Now I'm up here putting things in my suitcase and I begin to
feel ridiculous. This reminds me of a scene in a C-movie.

But Mom will be down there on the porch talking to him,
saying, Now Jack, you know how Sandy is, and the two of you
don't get along, but, etc., etc. She'll be busily smoothing the
whole thing over. So I listen, but I don't hear a word from
downstairs. What's going on? That's her role, to smooth things
over: *she's not smoothing things over,* what's going on? So I
keep on packing. Pretty soon the suitcase is all packed and I
still don't hear any voices downstairs.

Now I have to go down there with my suitcase. My father's
still out on the porch, but he's alone; my mother is sitting in
the living room. As I come down the stairs, she says to me, Can
I drive you to the bus?

Is it true? Have I heard the words properly? Yes, no way to get around them. With those seven words she defines her loyalty, her limits, her self-interest, her temperamental proclivities. That phrase is a masterpiece. The inevitability of it! The many layers of significance. At once simple and pithy, it does the job.

When I recover sufficiently to speak, I manage a belligerent Absolutely not! I'll take a taxi!

Then I lean down to the screened window that separates the living room from the porch where my father's swinging back and forth, and I come close and say, loudly, Do we really have to play this scene? He acts as if he doesn't hear me.

So I let my mother drive me to the bus.

On the way, I'm ranting in the car, saying, How can he really believe that nonsense he's talking about Nixon's innocence! I can't understand why he's saying those outrageous things! And she says, Of course he believes what he's saying. *I* certainly do.

There isn't anything to do but leave. I decide right now to go to New York City on the Greyhound, and I announce (not to be dismissed so summarily), When I get back I'll come to see you before I go on to California.

So I go to New York City where I have business to transact and several old friendships to renew. My time there is tolerably pleasant, and when I come back to Columbus, just an hour before I'm due at the airport to fly back to California, I get Nyla to drive me to my parents' house, where she insists on waiting in the car. I've called beforehand, and the excuse is that I am going to pick up some old pictures. We have to have an excuse: it isn't possible to say we are going to try to make up. So we sit and look at the snapshots, my mother and me, at this very dining room table where the blasphemy occurred, while my father paces like a disgruntled bear behind us.

Here is little Sandy sitting on the back step in her sunsuit, age two. Here are my sister, brother and I lined up stiffly against the living room wall looking like the czar's children staring down the barrels of a firing squad. My mother and I ponder two family dog pictures: this is Ham and this is Freddy, beings immured forever in our hearts. Is that blur in the background my cousin Carolyn? Honeysuckle perfume wafts seductively in through the screened windows, as it has and ever shall in Columbus in the spring.

When it is time to go, I decide to make a gesture of reconciliation. What have I got to lose?

I hug my father. He embraces me with arms of heavy wood, saying, Be a good girl.

Then I go to hug my mother, and I murmur to her, Be a good girl.

I always am, she replies.

And I leave, and have not returned.

Charm School

"I'd be careful about going too far up that way," the woman
says to Ellen. "There's a man up that way—a real sicky."

Ellen glances up the beach to where the figure of a man is visible in the thin fog, and two dogs leaping near him in the surf.

But the woman shakes her head. "No, he's wandering around
up on the cliffs. I mean, some of these guys I don't mind, but
this one scared me!" She gestures as she talks, and the wrinkles
in her forehead knot. "I was sitting there reading my paper
when he climbed down off the cliff. He came over and asked me
if I wanted some company. I said, 'No, I do not!' He just stood
there, and then he said, 'Show me your nipples.' "

Ellen and the woman exchange a look of shock, and then the
woman mimes her anger, lifting a clenched fist and pushing
away from her body with it. "Well, I turned to him and I said,
'You go away! Get away from here!' "

Ellen looks up to search the cliffs for a glimpse of him. They rise steeply from the beach, their packed sand ocher and tan and sienna, and on top the grass spikes up like hair.

"A real sicky. You know, if I were a young girl I'd expect to be approached, but I'm an older lady!"

When the woman has gone, Ellen stands looking in the opposite direction, back toward the Cliff House, but the tide is so high there that the beach is covered with water. No chance of going that way.

"Damn!" she says.

Lowering her head, she begins walking slowly along under the cliffs. "He's not going to drive me away!" she decides, and shoves her fists deep into the pockets of her jacket. But already the knowledge of his presence has slid like a screen between her and her surroundings. Thoughts rise in her like garbage from the bottom of a pond—sights she would rather forget, stories told by women in the coffee room at work, by her other friends. And she thinks of children. At what young age will a girl child hear that husky, whispered "Hey . . . look!" and turn to see the man in the darkened doorway, the man back among the trees, the man in the window. It is her own adolescent self she would like to shield against what happened long ago. But the memory is a hot probe in her.

Ellen kicks at a piece of seaweed shaped like the brown rubber bulb of a syringe. Scuffing her feet in the sand, she glances at the cliffs which rear up, gouged and grooved by weather. Is that a movement up there, or is it just the wind ruffling the grass? She watches for a time, seeing no one.

It is years since she has thought of Zangaro. She plods down the beach, her hands clasped behind her, knowing it is the man up on the cliffs who has plunged her into these thoughts, and hating him for it.

The summer Ellen was seventeen, a Charm School and Modeling School opened in Minneapolis where she lived with her family. No such establishment had ever existed in that solid and businesslike town, and a lot of press coverage was given to its offices in a downtown hotel and to its owner, a Mr. Henri Zangaro from New York City.

From these newspaper articles Ellen's parents got the idea that Mr. Zangaro's charm school would be the answer to what they defined as her "problem." She had not been popular in the high school from which she had just graduated; in fact, she had been miserable and ignored for those four years. Ellen knew it had been because she came from the wrong part of town each day to attend that school in a prosperous suburb, because her father was not a doctor or a businessman but a machinist in a factory, because she wore cheap nylon sweaters while the others wore cashmere or suede.

But she had no words to tell her parents this. Surely they must have known it themselves. Yet now they wanted to help her, having watched her suffer through those four years—and especially they were anxious that she should succeed in finding a husband.

So Ellen's mother, with unusual initiative, inquired by phone of the Charm School to see if they needed a typist, and arranged that Ellen could work out her tuition at the school by doing typing at night after her regular job in an office downtown. Secretly she was hurt that her parents saw her as deficient and in need of fixing up, yet she was grateful to them too for trying to help her. She would not, herself, have chosen such a school, but since it had been arranged, she agreed to go.

Mr. Zangaro had what amounted to a harem. He was surrounded by young women whom he handled and groomed, cutting their hair, giving them lessons in makeup, telling them how to stand, to sit, how to act toward men ("When a man is lighting your cigarette, look up into his eyes over the flame."), what kind of girdle to buy, what clothes to wear. Obediently, Ellen did all she was told to do, feeling strangely dislocated.

And since she was there with Mr. Zangaro in the office several hours every evening typing the promotional letters, he talked to her about himself. He had grown up in Hell's Kitchen in New York, had started out by making sketches on the street and various other hustles. By sheer ruthlessness and a crude charm that came mostly from his sexual curiosity and erotic awareness of women, he had worked his way up in the beauty business. And of course he changed his first name of Gaetano to the requisite French name, and became Henri.

A short, square man, with stubby hands, he was tough, and proud of how far he had raised himself from his poor beginnings. His little eyes were sharp and knowing. He had a wide mouth, with lips that were sensual and cruel, over wide-spaced, tobacco-stained teeth. It was a mouth that fell most naturally into a sneer.

Sometimes as Ellen was typing he would stand peering at her and then say, "Ellen, you need a trim. Come in the back." And obediently she went behind the partition with him and sat down in the barber's chair. Then he would clip and pat her hair. She saw him in the mirror, his little eyes squinted against the smoke from the Old Gold that almost always hung on his lip, gazing proprietarily at her head. He talked about the models he had known in New York—one in particular who had been a stunning creature, chased by numbers of men, who would have none of them because she was a lesbian. He shook his head. The idea fascinated him. This is life, he was saying to Ellen, I'm telling you what life is about. And then he would go into one of his lectures. "Something like a pimple on a girl's nose—just one little pimple—can turn a man off completely." He talked about his wife, the latest one, whom he had acquired when he came to Minnesota. "She has a master's degree in literature," he told Ellen. And it was obvious what a triumph it had been for him to marry this woman who had "culture." She was now at home bearing his children—two so far.

In these hours when they were alone in his office, there was something established between them. It was something Ellen did not seek and did not want, but *he* was in charge there, and she had been so successfully trained into respect for authority, beginning with her father, that her only manner of resistance was to withdraw. In this situation in which he controlled the space and the interchange between them, withdrawing did no good. During classes or when others were in the office, he was brisk and businesslike to her, but when they were alone, he drew her into his circle of energy, played on her innocence, talked

mostly of sex: he was certain it was the moving force for everyone. He was inexhaustibly fascinated by it.

Rough and cynical, he let it be known that he was honoring
Ellen by treating her as a friend. And he was going to help her
move up in the world. One day his prize pupil came in to visit.
She was just back from New York City where she worked as a
photographer's model. She was almost six feet tall and weighed
115 pounds. A photograph, Zangaro had told Ellen, puts on
twenty pounds. So obviously a photographer's model must
be at least twenty pounds underweight. Ellen found this
young woman distressing to look at. Poised, elegant, she was
so emaciated that the veins stood out on her wrists and ankles
like blue worms over the bones. She was strangely languid,
speaking in a slow flat voice. She told Zangaro she was in town
to get her teeth capped and see her family, and she brought out
some folded papers from her big model's bag and showed him
the magazine spreads in which she had been featured.

When she had gone, Zangaro said, "She makes a lot of money.
You could do it too. You've got the bones."

Ellen didn't want to do it. What she really wanted was to go
to college, even though her parents had not let her take the college preparatory course in high school but had insisted she take
the commercial course. That meant that while the others studied
Latin and French she studied typewriting and basic bookkeeping.
She did not blame her parents, they were merely being practical;
the training had made it easy for her to get a job as a typist.

A visitor who came often to the office, though he seemed to
have no particular business to transact, was an enormous meaty
man with slicked down platinum-bleached hair—a professional
wrestler. Zangaro became almost obsequious in his presence,
laughing with hysterical urgency at the jokes the man made, saying over and over to anyone who was present, "Isn't he a gas?"
This behavior puzzled Ellen, for Zangaro maintained a consistently tough and sneering manner with everyone else.

"I went out with this girl," began the man, with a smirk on
his beefy face to indicate this was to be a funny story. "She
was a hunchback. I didn't like that, so I took her to a graveyard

and I dug a grave and put the hunch in it. And that was the end of that."

"Dug a grave!" sputtered Zangaro. "Put the hunch in it!" And he rocked with harsh laughter. "You hear that, Ellen?" He gripped the big man's arm, doubled over with hilarity.

Ellen stared at them, repelled. She tried to smile, but couldn't. She saw nothing funny in what the man had said, and it only made her more aware that this place was alien territory. In another few weeks her charm course, and thus the job, would be finished, and she would never have to sit here again.

Then one evening the daytime secretary was there doing a special project, using the desk, and Zangaro said, "Okay, let's go upstairs to work, Ellen. I wanta go over this next batch of letters with you." He opened the door, told the secretary to hold all calls for the next hour, and went briskly out into the hall.

Ellen followed, wondering where they were going, glanced back through the glass door at the secretary sitting at the front desk. She followed Zangaro into the elevator, where he stood gazing sternly before him, in a hurry, businesslike. At the seventh floor the elevator stopped. They got out, and Ellen followed Zangaro down the hotel corridor past numbered doors. At one of them he stopped, inserted a key, opened it and motioned her in.

Ellen had never been in a hotel room. When her family traveled to see relatives, they covered the distance in one day; they were not the kind of people who stayed in hotels.

"Phew! Hot!" Zangaro said, and went to open the window.

The room was dull, perfunctory, furnished with a double bed, two chairs, a small glass-topped desk. Traffic noise came in through the window Zangaro had opened.

Ellen stood holding the papers they had come to look at, feeling extremely uncomfortable. That intimacy that had been established between her and Zangaro seemed suddenly stifling. But he was arranging the two chairs before the desk, his motions quick and matter-of-fact.

It was a summer evening, one of those in which the heat does not lift when the sun goes down. Ellen had been at work all day in an office. Her clothes felt sticky and too small; her feet had swollen a little, puffing up so that the edges of her pumps cut into her flesh. Her girdle and hose bound her damply, the stockings pulling behind the knees.

She sat down in the chair next to Zangaro, seeing his rough brown hair, his rough lined skin filmed with sweat. There were brown hairs curling on the backs of his stubby hands.

He explained to her what he wanted in the letters, how he wanted them to look. They worked for about fifteen minutes, and then he sank back in his chair and pulled out a handkerchief to wipe his forehead. His suit coat was open, his tie pulled down from his unbuttoned collar.

"Jesus, my legs hurt," he said, gripping his short thick fingers on his knees, rubbing them. "I been standing all day today." And then he turned his chair to face her. "Here, see what you can do."

She looked at him, not understanding.

"C'mon, give 'em a rub. Help me out." He reached to lift her hands and place them on his knees. "That's right, rub. Come on."

His manner said, This is all perfectly ordinary. There is nothing unusual about it.

Ellen sat with her hands on his knees, looking at his face. He was staring past her, his lips curved into a disdainful smile. The sound of automobiles came through the opened window, the twilight was a transparent grey blue. She felt the moisture on her sides under her clothes.

Slowly, she began to rub his knees. "Harder," he said, "dig in a little." She tightened her fingers, kneading.

"Aaah, that's good," he said, and he closed his eyes and leaned back in the chair. "Right. That's right."

Ellen looked up past his spread thighs to his short torso relaxed in the chair, his forearms propped on the chair arms.

The room filled up with a silence then, under the traffic hum. He looked as if he were sleeping.

She rubbed his knees.

"Higher," he said, "up a little higher. Ah, yes, that's good."

Her hands moved now on the big muscles of his thighs. It was as if she were hypnotized, part of her standing aside to watch herself do this. She tried to think of a way to stop, but each time she slowed her hands, he said, "No, don't stop. Aaah, feels good." He did not open his eyes to look at her, he did not move, his hands did not touch her. Instinctively she knew that if she stopped or objected he would laugh at her, he would make her feel like a fool for imagining this to be something that it wasn't.

She kneaded the thighs, watched the hands reach to unbuckle the belt, pull the zipper down a little while he sighed.

"Higher," he said, and she moved her hands up a little more, closer to his groin. Now she could see the thick ridge there.

He began to breathe strangely, a kind of snorting in his nose, that he was trying to control, and the swelling under the zipper of his pants got bigger.

Ellen was locked here, caught between what she was seeing and his nonchalant manner that forbade her to define it. She sweated, and her back hurt from leaning over his legs, but she was afraid to break the silence, to break the spell, was afraid of his contempt.

His lips had parted a little now, she could see the tongue move across the stained teeth. But his eyes remained closed, and there was something so distant about his face that it seemed he was not there at all. How could she make an objection to someone who was not there to hear her?

Then, in one smooth motion, he drew the zipper all the way down, grasped her hands and thrust them inside the opening.

Ellen gasped. Her hands fumbled against hot hairy skin, the round hard shaft lying against the belly.

"No, like this," he muttered, from his distant, apparently sleeping face, and he took her fingers and curled them around that throbbing trunk of flesh, and moved them up and down, up and down.

Ellen struggled in confusion. He had stolen words from her, he had stolen true perception and will. Yet she knew what her hands felt—the skin moving loosely on the shaft, his buttocks subtly writhing. She heard his breath sputtering out through his lips. He was pretending with his face that nothing was happening.

She was frightened and repelled, but his face said, Nothing is happening, Absolutely nothing unusual is happening, while his short fingers gripped hers, pumping them up and down, up and down on his penis that stood up against his hairy belly like something that lived an independent life.

Then he gave a low "Unnnnnnh"—and his hands held hers still. She felt a pulsing in the flesh under her fingers and saw the whitish fluid spurt out the end and spread sticky and thick on the belly.

She looked up at Zangaro's face. It was blotched with dark color, the lips shone wet. But the eyes remained closed, and there was no expression but his usual stern scornful one.

Then his hands lifted carefully from hers, and she pulled her fingers away, unwinding them from the shaft of flesh that had become soft and fell to the side. She drew her hands back into her lap and sat there in amazement and shame. Her body was terribly hot, all her clothes constricting it. Her breath was shallow. Never before in her seventeen years had she seen a man's genitals. Her brothers and her father kept theirs discreetly hidden. Once when she had danced close with a boy she had felt him get hard down there. That was the extent of her sophistication.

Having zipped his pants, Mr. Zangaro was buckling his belt. Those small clever eyes were finally open, but they wore an expression of studied casualness, and they did not look at Ellen. He turned his chair back to the desk, and lifted the papers there.

Ellen sat watching him, her whole body uneasy. And to escape the sourness rising in her throat, she searched in her mind for some inkling of what would happen now. Glancing at the bed, she thought that what must happen now would be that he would "make love" to her. She had read a novel in which the older man initiated the young woman into sex; he was very gentle and afterwards he looked at her body and told her she was beautiful, and because he said so she knew she was a real woman at last. Was that what was going to happen between her and Zangaro now? Were they having an "affair"? All of this must mean that he loved and wanted her. It must mean that! She struggled to place the fantasy between herself and what she knew.

It was steamy hot and silent in the room, except for the quiet sounds of the papers being moved on the desk.

Zangaro cleared his throat, and Ellen felt the sound in her own body.

"Here," he said, "I think we'd better change this paragraph." He read, "For only $3.50 a session, you can learn the secrets of the most glamorous models. . .uh. . .no, mannequins. . .in the. . . uh. . .dazzling. . .whaddayou think of that, Ellen, dazzling okay? . . .uhm. . .in the dazzling world of high fashion." He bent over to write in the changes.

Ellen sat staring at his profile.

Briskly, he stacked the sheets, handed them to her. Her hands were so numb that she let the papers slip to the rug. He waited while she retrieved them. Then he stood up and said, "Mary should be done with the typewriter by now, and you can get started."

He went to the door, opened it, waited for her.

The room had filled with shadow. She sat staring at his figure by the door, could just make out the impatient arch of his eyebrows. Slowly she raised herself from the chair and walked across the room, past the bed, past him, and out into the hall.

When they entered the office downstairs, the secretary glanced up, examining Ellen with a knowing look. Ellen felt herself go scarlet.

"Let her get to work there, when you're finished," Zangaro said, and went off quickly into the back room.

That was so many long years ago. Yet the remembrance is vivid in Ellen—how she had not been able to meet the secretary's eyes. She had stood heavy and miserable, clutching the sheaf of papers, staring at the photographs of sleek women that lined the walls. And that evening, riding home on the bus, filled with self-loathing, she was repulsed by her own hands. She was repulsed by herself.

Now Ellen realizes how far up the beach she has wandered, below the looming cliffs. The man with the dogs is a tiny figure in

the mist far behind her. She looks out to where the waves curl
and foam in khaki water. Abruptly she glances up at the cliffs,
and sees there the upper body of a man, bent slightly forward,
watching her. She stops, and stands looking up. Yes, here where
there is no one else, she has become the prey. The man is too
high up to be clearly seen. He might as well be Zangaro in the
dim room, standing at the door.

Casually, Ellen moves up closer to the cliff, looking about her
at the debris strewn on the sand. When she glances up again, his
figure is gone, and she stoops to pick up the piece of wood she
has spotted. It is a heavy chunk of board, broken off from one
of the logs that roll in on the surf. And at its end is a rusty bolt
partially embedded.

She chooses a patch of warm sand up near the cliff and sits
down facing the sea, putting the piece of wood next to her.
Leaning back on stiffened arms, she watches the waves break
and smooth out and come sliding up the sand, glimmering silver
where the sun hits them.

Ellen is perfectly still inside. She smiles a bitter smile as she
remembers how years later she had heard that Zangaro sued his
wife for divorce, claiming she was a lesbian. How like him it
was. And how wonderfully ironic it would have been if the
woman *had* been a lesbian. But Ellen doubts that. More likely
it was his own imagination and weird desire that had concocted
the story.

She lowers her head to rest on her knees, and tries to listen to
the sounds about her, to enter, if only for a few moments, into
the natural universe. Under the shoosh of each succeeding wave,
is the steady dull roar, like a giant engine. If Ellen were not so
familiar with it she might look up to scan the sky, expecting to
see a plane. But she knows it is the voice of the ocean, inter-
minably speaking. Recognizing it, she cannot enter it now,
for in her head lurks the possibility of what the next few
minutes will bring.

It is not long before she begins to hear a scraping and scram-
bling on the cliff behind her. Her whole body listens as she sees
a yellow rock roll down onto the sand.

Then she can feel the presence beside her, and she turns her head to look.

Above shiny brown loafers are neatly pressed wool trousers, a white shirt and wide tie under a tweed sports jacket. His face is pink and his thick salt-and-pepper eyebrows sit like little caterpillars up high on his forehead. His hair is black with patches of grey in it, stylishly cut, full but not too long, as might befit an appliance salesman or a TV personality. His anxious eyes blink at Ellen.

"Hel-*lo*," he says brightly, and he reaches down to his fly, which is already open, and pulls out a short uncircumcized cock and fleshy balls, all of an odd pasty color. He holds this soft pile of genitals in the palms of his hands, offering it to Ellen like a doughy bouquet.

She gets quickly to her feet, clutching the piece of wood.

Leaning forward, she shouts into the sea wind. "You must really want to get yourself in trouble, doing that, you must want someone to call the police on you, I could go get them right now, I could bring them back here and they'd find you and lock you up, is that what you want? Is it?"

He stands leaning his shoulders back away from her, his pelvis rocked forward. His pink face is a mask of humiliation.

"No," he says, "I want a woman."

"Oh, really?!" Ellen throws up her hand. "You want a woman. This is how you expect to find a woman?"

"Yes," he says stubbornly.

"You don't want a woman, you just want someone to *look* at you, isn't that right!"

He scrunches his neck down into the collar of his shirt and does not answer. And Ellen realizes that he has been getting what he wanted: she has been looking at him.

Lifting the stick, she takes a threatening step toward him, expecting him to move away from her. But he simply cringes, and his face with its fuzzy eyebrows perched up high has on it an expression that says, I know I am despicable. Whatever you may do to me will not be sufficient to punish me for what I am.

Ellen is stopped. She can not bear looking in his eyes, which are so deep with self-despising. He makes her experience some part of herself which she does not want to own, and she is held there, bound to him in weakness, disgust.

She drops the piece of wood on the sand. Going around him, she begins to walk toward the parking lot.

"Hey!" he calls softly, but Ellen goes on without looking back, her mind already turning to her house, the friend with whom she lives. She plods away from him down the beach, leaving him with his hands cupped at his crotch, his face obscenely beseeching.

The Notebooks of Leni Clare

PART I

Living Separately

"So was it good?" A careful question, asked without looking at Gretchen, as Leni hung her blouse in the closet.

They had arrived home at the same time, coming from opposite ends of the alley to meet at the curved iron grillework of the outer door of their building. Now, inside the apartment, Leni was changing the clothes she wore to her office job for blue jeans and a loose shirt. Gretchen leaned in the doorway of the bedroom, her canvas carrying bag on the floor before her.

"How can I describe it to you, Leni? I know none of it means anything to you . . . but for me, just the quiet, the sunshine on the grass, the birds in the morning . . . ."

Leni fastened the waistband of her jeans, thinking, Yes, and a new lover too. *That* you're not mentioning. She turned to look at Gretchen, whose hair was tousled, her body relaxed in that

soft yielding attitude she always had when she came back from
a few days in the country.

"I mean I was just *happy* there. And I realized I haven't been
just plain happy in a year."

As Gretchen talked on about the healing effects of her experience in the country, Leni began to think about dinner. Maybe
an omelet—mushrooms and onion and broccoli and cheese. So
much anxiety these days. So much that is new. Maybe enchila-
das—a special treat—do we have any tomato sauce? And what
will it be like when we move up to the country *together*? The
time was coming very soon, Leni more and more uncertain
about it but determined to go.

Gretchen opened the sliding double doors between the bedroom and the front room, and went through them to look at
the plants hanging in the bay windows. She pulled off a dead
leaf here, arranged an errant frond there, felt the earth in the
pots for moisture.

Maybe even eggplant parmesan, thought Leni. Something
complicated that would take time and effort. She was looking
at Gretchen's shoulders, at her thick black hair laced with grey.
Then she began to hear what Gretchen was saying, and her
breath caught in her throat.

"It'll be better for me. I think it'll be much better."

Leni took a step toward her.

"You mean you don't want . . . ?"

Gretchen leaned over a large plant with wide flat leaves, her
back to Leni, as she said, "I want to be up there by myself. I
need to be alone."

Leni felt as if she had been kicked in the chest.

"But we decided . . . ."

Gretchen turned, her face somber. "I know. But I realized
yesterday when I was sitting out in the meadow that I need to
be there just by myself, to sort out my life."

She stood amid the jungle of her many plants, a wiry woman
with determined mouth and dark troubled eyes. Leni lifted her
hands toward Gretchen.

"I don't want to make you feel bad," Gretchen said.

Leni drew back her hands and clasped them over her mid-section. "I suppose it's because of *her*, is that right?"

"No, no." And Gretchen was beside her, holding her arm. "It's not about that, Leni, believe me. It's about *me*, and what *I* need!"

She enfolded Leni in a hug, and Leni clung, turning her face into Gretchen's hair.

"You know I'll miss you every day," Gretchen said against her ear. "It's just for a while. We'll see each other as often as possible."

Slowly Leni stepped back from her, looking at her mouth, the darker shadows on her pale brownish skin, the sharp hook of her nose. Gretchen's eyes shone with pain as well as excitement and a kind of joy that Leni had not seen for a long time. It remind-ed her of their first year together. The memory caused her to look away and take a long quaky breath. There had been too much crying lately: she would push that need down inside her-self.

"Why?" she asked. "Tell me again, *why*?"

* * *

The next morning Leni was furious. How could Gretchen change her mind so quickly, she fumed as she stood waiting for the bus that would take her to work. After all, they had planned for months that she too would stay in the country house. She had gotten herself set for it, and that had not been easy, since she would have had to quit her job and did not know if she could find another up there; she had worried too about her abil-ity to cope with the isolation of rural living. And it had been so much against her politics to escape to the country. They had ar-gued about it often, Gretchen ranting, "Oh yeah, you prefer this neighborhood where you risk getting your head beat in if you go out after dark! You like stepping over the bums and winos on the street. You find that cheerful, right? That makes you feel good!" And Leni would reply doggedly, "It reminds me of how most people in the world have to live."

But finally, under the constant pressure from Gretchen, she had agreed to go. Now she would have to readjust her plans and expectations. Still, she felt a little spring of relief, the intimation that after these weeks of indecision she would no longer have to endure Gretchen's one day wanting one thing, the next day something entirely opposite; not have to live with it and adjust to it practically hour by hour as she had been doing. The idea of Gretchen's living elsewhere, painful as it was, seemed to offer some promise of peace.

So Gretchen would move. That evening they looked at each other in surprise. Not to live together! And the most insignificant elements of their shared lives suddenly carried great weights of meaning. Gretchen, bringing the grocery bags down the long hall of their apartment to the kitchen, as she had done for four years, realized she would do that no more. All at once this humble act seemed the quintessence of providing, of nurturing herself and Leni, and she stood over the bulging bags set on the kitchen table, transfixed.

In her desk drawer Leni found some questionnaires about menstruation each of them had filled out. In answer to the question: "How is she different around her period?" Gretchen had written, "She needs more affection, quiet times with me." And Leni felt Gretchen's caring for her. How could she, then, go to live somewhere else? Not to *be* there for Leni! When Leni had her period next time Gretchen would be in Guerneville, fifty miles away.

Awaking from a violent dream, Leni turned to curve her body around Gretchen's in the bed. "If I died in an accident on the highway, would you care?" she whispered.

Gretchen, half asleep, muttered "Of course I would. Don't be silly."

But Leni swam in a sea of self-pity, thinking of her ID card where it listed whom to contact in case of emergency. Whose name would she put there now that she had been abandoned?

Both of them were aware of the many ways in which Gretchen had taken care of Leni, dealing with the car, the landlord, the fuse box, the neighbors. For a long while it had bolstered Gretchen's ego to do those things; then it was habit between them and impossible to change. Now how will I manage? Leni wondered. When she was married, although she worked to provide half the income and did all the cooking, cleaning and washing, her husband had repaired things in the apartment, fixed the car, and assumed a certain authority over their lives. Then when she became a lesbian she sought out women who were capable and used to dealing with the world. From the age of fifteen Leni had earned a living, but she did not want to take more responsibility than that for her life. It had been easier to find someone who enjoyed tinkering and making arrangements and tidying up, who liked to plan and manage. Now she was scared.

But at moments she felt accepting of the change, especially since Gretchen was still here with her. What did it mean, after all? They would still be lovers, their relationship would be as strong as ever, they would simply be living separately for a while. When she looked at it that way Leni could feel relatively cheerful about it.

One evening she took up the latest notebook she was using. For a year now she had been keeping a journal in stenographers notebooks brought home from the office. Sometimes she wrote while riding the bus to work, in a jerky scrawl, her left hand cupped to shield her words from the passengers standing above her; sometimes she wrote at home, as she was doing now, sitting on the mattress in the middle room.

> So we were at the table and I was saying Hey, all I need is my tacos (which I was eating) and my cats, if I have those I'm happy. And I looked up and saw that Gretchen looked really crushed. She said, You just want to get rid of me.
> Well I felt pretty bad then and I told her how sorry I was. I mean I am going to miss her at dinnertimes, when she's not here.
> Seems like both of us are real sensitive right now.

They began moving Gretchen's things to the country carload by carload on the weekends. And Gretchen began dressing like a country woman, wearing jeans and plaid shirt and down-filled vest, a flop-brimmed black felt hat with a braided headband. She looked jaunty and rugged, and the picture was complete when she traded in her car for a big old station wagon. On the

dashboard she arranged feathers and shells and small bits of
driftwood, and when she got in the car to drive to the country
she always lit a stick of incense. Never mind that this vehicle got
8 miles to the gallon of gas and was so old the floor under the
passenger seat had rusted out.

She spoke with disdain of "city energy," and when they
arrived at the Guerneville cabin in among the redwoods she fell
silent. When Leni talked, Gretchen would walk out of the room
or endure the monologue with a look of strained forbearance.
"You talk too much," she told Leni finally. "If you'll just be
quiet you can feel the energy here. The trees. The air."

Leni went outside so that Gretchen would not see the sudden
tears that wet her face. It seemed everything she did was wrong
now. She was a symbol of the city, apparently; of all that was
oppressive and anti-nature. She stood looking up at the giant
trees that shut out the sun from the cabin. Down here at their
roots the air was damp and shadowed. She shivered, thinking of
what Donna, Gretchen's new lover, had said, as reported to her
by Gretchen: that the country is the place for spirituality, the
city is the place for politics. Leni reacted strongly against such
formulations. She believed that the most spiritually advanced
people were probably working as waitresses in big city diners, or
as janitors in giant apartment houses. They were the simple people who were able to be fully present and full of love in the most
crowded and miserable of conditions. At Gretchen's urging, she
had gone to a meditation circle in San Francisco led by a very
down-to-earth young woman. At one point during the evening
this woman had said, "If you can't meditate on the subway, forget it," and Leni had sat up straight in recognition, grinning at
her.

Still, the air here was wonderful, damp and cool, carrying
odors of bark and leaves. Leni breathed deeply, swung her arms,
put back her head to look up past the red brown massive tree
trunks tapering to delicate fans of leaves against a bright cloud-
less sky. Around her there was a silence that seemed to rest in
layers from the cushiony earth up to the tops of the trees.

Back inside the cabin she helped Gretchen sweep the mouse
dung from the floors, clean out the fireplace, hang her pictures

on the plasterboard walls. The cabin was built of planks painted
a dark brown to blend in among the trees. The rooms smelled
of rotting wood.

Gretchen had set up her little makeshift altar of bricks and
board and a scarf in a corner of the living room, and now when
Leni thought it was time to eat dinner, Gretchen lit the candles
on the altar and stuck a smoking stick of incense upright in a
bowl of sand.

"I'm going to meditate for half an hour," she told Leni.
"Join me if you like."

The invitation was so casual, so impersonal, that Leni felt
once again Gretchen's eagerness to be alone up here. She
watched Gretchen sit down cross-legged on a pillow, tucking her
heels into her crotch, place a hand on each knee, and close her
eyes. And as the silence settled, Leni looked out the windows
to the green and brown of the trees, the air faintly green tinged.
Being here was a little like being underwater, the house sub-
merged in a ferny pond.

She moved restlessly in her chair, remembering how upset she
had been when Gretchen had begun this meditation practice a
few months ago with the encouragement of Donna and some
other country women. Leni thought of it as escapism, fuzzy
mindedness, superstition; and it seemed ludicrously inappropri-
ate for Gretchen, who had always been more connected to every-
day necessities than Leni. But she did not dare object, for there
was already so much resentment between them. Only once did
she express her disapproval. Gretchen, who had been studying
the cards of the Tarot deck, had persuaded Leni to come into
the middle room of their apartment to sit on the mattress and
submit to a reading. At a certain hour of afternoon the sun
slipped between their building and the tenement behind them to
fall through the window onto the mattress. It rested like a warm
hand on Leni's thigh as she watched Gretchen place the cards.
Gretchen's hair gleamed blue black in the light, her face was
dark and peaceful. With her gypsy coloring she looked just right
bending over the cards, and Leni saw her as she never had before.
Her stomach tightened as she realized that this had been part of
Gretchen as long as she'd known her; behind that strict practi-

cality hid a tendency to wonder about psychic phenomena, to
puzzle on spiritual matters. Now, clearly, this leaning toward
mysticism was developing, coming out to be real in the world.
In those few minutes Leni saw Gretchen as a remote creature focused on her inner self, a dreamer, a seer. Frightened, she struck
out at Gretchen, talking in a harsh rejecting voice about this
"decadent crap" that Gretchen brought home from Donna. She
paced and railed, and came up against the full force of Gretchen's
quick anger, and they plunged into another of their bitter fights.

But today, in the Guerneville cabin, Leni sat quietly. She was
hungry. She did not dare go to the kitchen, however, fearing
her noise might disturb Gretchen. Like a cowed child, she kept
still, staring now at the side of Gretchen's face, so closed to her.
This face with its thin lips, its aquiline nose, the dark eyelashes
long on the cheeks, had always drawn Leni; she would feel herself reaching to touch, to kiss. Leni had loved Gretchen's nose
especially: it seemed exotic, handsome and definite, a flamboy-
ant gesture. Now Leni found Gretchen more beautiful than
usual, as she sat without moving, her face peaceful. Leni
watched in helpless passivity.

* * *

When she came back to San Francisco, Leni stood in the alley
before their building and felt how far away this was from the
small brown cabin in the redwoods. Here one old Victorian
apartment house merged with the next; each bay window was
hung with blinds or drapes or plants in macrame slings; behind
each lived a family. Iron gates protected the entrances. At the
Guerrero Street end of the alley stood a large building that was
a treatment center for the kind of alcoholics who propped themselves in doorways down on Sixth Street. Cleaned up, still these
men were red faced, scarred and shambling. At the other end of
the alley stood a factory in which women, mostly Chinese, Fili-
pina and Latina, sewed shirts and pants. In the vacant lot across
from Leni's front door, old tires were piled, and a rusted metal
bedframe tilted above them.

Standing here, Leni felt the crush of people, the close-packed
humanity, the continual activity. She had always liked that feel-

ing. While she had grown up in the outskirts of a town in New Jersey, since she came west with her husband at age twenty she had lived in San Francisco, usually in the Mission District. Now she was thirty-three, and still it reassured her to live so closely surrounded by people, even while she was aware of the toll it took, the physical tension necessary to fend off the noise and deal with hostile or threatening encounters on the street, the mental effort involved in maintaining her equilibrium within the crises, the anguish and despair and occasional wild delight, the passionate daily experience of other people. Close behind her building stood an ancient apartment house, a large grey wooden structure rising above a narrow, weed-filled vacant lot On warm days the men who lived there sat on the windowsills and drank beer, talking in low sullen voices, while the women moved in the rooms, cooking, tending the children. When Leni went out to water her few tomato plants, she could feel the men's stares, their attention a weight on her shoulders.

Leni opened the iron gate and came into the entranceway of her building. She let the gate go, hearing it slam behind her, and walked past the first door. From behind it she heard the shrieks of children. Opening her own door she came into the inner hall. When they first moved in, Gretchen had hung prints on the wall all the way down the hallway to the kitchen. Leni glanced at them, so neatly matted. They were taken from a portfolio of drawings by women, an effort to show strong or nontraditional images of women. And Leni knew that Gretchen, who had only recently begun to think in feminist terms, had hung the pictures to honor Leni's commitment. Leni felt a fullness in her throat, now, looking at the prints.

Never in four years had she imagined that she and Gretchen would not live together. The idea shook the very foundations of her sense of safety in the world.

Still, she was able to write in her notebook:

We're moving Gretchen up to the country. Kind of like she's moving out inch by inch. Sometimes I want her to hurry up and leave so I can just be alone to think about all this stuff that's happened.

In September Gretchen had gone to a gathering of women in
the country, a retreat where, she told Leni, they were to engage
in something called "guided meditation" and problem solving.
She returned to inform Leni that she had made love with one of
the women there and intended to continue seeing her. "Problem
solving, my foot!" Leni had said bitterly. "Does a new lover
make everything different?" But her terror went deep.

Already there were difficulties between them over Gretchen's
desire to move out of the city, over their different financial situations; almost everything in their lives had become cause for
conflict. This was only another blow. Gretchen assured Leni
that her relationship with Donna was very limited compared to
the depth of her feelings for Leni and the intimacy engendered
by their four years together. Leni thought that was probably
true, yet she suffered intensely in the following months when
Gretchen went out to Sonoma County to be with Donna for
days and nights at a time. One advantage, Leni realized, to their
living apart now, would be that she would not know which
nights Gretchen spent with Donna.

They agreed that Leni should not be at the house while
Gretchen officially moved out, in order to save her that pathetic
wandering about after somebody who is packing to leave, that
wistful waving from the front window as the loaded car pulls off
down the alley. So Leni went out to dinner with a friend. Later
that night, alone in the apartment, she sat propped up in bed,
and wrote in her notebook:

> December 15
>   It's very late now, seems a lifetime since I came home. Funny,
> I'd been having a good time, but when I got inside the door I
> started to cry. Then I found Gretchen's note, and that was a little
> better, knowing she'd call. Didn't feel like sleeping, so I've been
> wrapping her xmas presents and listening to the Holly Near tape
> she left me.
>   Got to go to sleep. Feels so strange.

The next morning when she awoke, she did not allow herself
to lie in bed but got up quickly to pull the covers tight over the
twin pillows, went into the bathroom to shower, and in her bath-

robe went down the hall to the green, high-ceilinged kitchen. Here she fed the one cat who was left and put the water on for coffee. On the bulletin board next to the sink were hung leaflets and political announcements and the notes left by friends who had stayed overnight. "Dear Leni and Gretchen, I loved sleeping in your middle room. Thanks for the hospitality."

Leni looked away, and she felt something not so much hollowed out as scraped out, a space in her head and one in her chest, dug out by some jagged instrument, existing raw and empty.

She lowered her head, thinking, *This hurts,* wondering, Will I feel this all day every day? She let her chin sink to her chest and stared at the counter, thinking, Why *can't* people stay together and care about each other? Why did she have to run away? The questions fed into a deep self-pitying sense of betrayal, Leni an innocent child abandoned. People don't even try to work things out anymore, she told herself, and she experienced a huge enveloping nostalgia for the life she and Gretchen had lived here together.

But the water was boiling and in half an hour she had to be out of the apartment and down at the bus stop. Leni roused herself, and entered into the routine of making coffee, frying an egg. On this day, with Gretchen gone, it seemed even more important than usual to get to work on time. And she's *not* gone, Leni told herself as she sat down at the kitchen table with her fried egg on a plate, she's only living somewhere else for a time.

That evening, she was very tired from the steady typing that was all she was given to do at this latest job, and tired also from a curious maneuver she had engaged in all day of studiously *not* thinking of Gretchen, not imagining the empty apartment, not looking forward to the weekend when she would be alone. Now she sat in the kitchen drinking a beer, hoping it would dull her, knowing she had the second can right here if the first one didn't do the trick.

Sounds from next door came pounding through the wall as a fight started, the children began to yell, and the music increased in volume. Ever since the new neighbors had moved

in two weeks ago, this noise had gone on almost continually,
late into the night. Leni and Gretchen had not understood
how little children could still be shrieking and running up and
down the hall of the apartment at two a.m. Gretchen had
twice gone out to knock at the door and ask for quiet. Each
time a child had answered. Each time the noise had calmed
temporarily and then taken up again. Leni had seen one or
another of the children at the window, on the sidewalk.
They were skinny, round-headed, big-eyed children with
dark brown skin and sweet shy hesitant smiles. Once on a Sunday Leni had seen them leaving the house with their mother, a
small pretty woman who herded them along with a look of tender pride on her otherwise strained and timid face. They had
been dressed up in colorful clothes, three girls and two boys,
none above the age of twelve, Leni judged, and their faces shone
with pleasure and excitement as they walked with their mother
down the sidewalk, jockeyed to hold her hand, grasp a corner of
her coat.

Leni had thought they were beautiful. And now as she sat
assaulted by the noise, hearing a chair crash to the floor beyond
the wall and the loud argument continue, she wondered how
she would be able to tolerate this. It had been a little easier
when Gretchen had been here, Gretchen standing between her
and the uproar. Now she was totally at its mercy. It was equally audible in the bedroom, the bathroom, the middle room, and
now that they had broken the window in the front door, the
noise would be even louder at the front of the apartment.

The beer was dulling her senses somewhat. She finished it off
and considered preparing dinner. But she had no appetite, and
the thought of making dinner just for herself, sitting here at the
table alone to eat it, saddened her. Well, maybe she would just
put the groceries away, drink the other beer, and eat later.

She had contemplated calling the landlord about the racket
next door but had decided not to when she discovered what the
situation was. Gretchen had learned from the oldest daughter
that the mother left each evening to go to a job cleaning offices
in a downtown building, and she came back in the morning just
in time to get the children off to school. So the children were

alone there all night, with no one to discipline them or put them to bed.

Leni took the second beer with her down the hall to the bedroom. She stretched out on the bed and stared at the plants hanging at the bay windows and standing in wrought iron holders on the floor. Gretchen had asked Leni if she minded taking care of them, as there was not enough light at the country house. Leni watered them and tried to pay attention to them, but she was not attuned to plants, and while she experienced pleasant sensations in their presence, she almost never actually looked at one of them or focused her mind on it. Gretchen had patted and pruned and repotted them, talked to them, examined them minutely.

When Leni looked at them, as she was doing now, she saw a leafy screen over her thoughts. Her mind at the moment was occupied with the children next door, whose clamor invaded her house, her sleep, her every waking moment at home. She did not want to tell the landlord about them because he might kick them out. Leni could imagine how difficult it must be for a Black single mother to find an apartment for herself and five children. Or the landlord, discovering that the children were alone there at night, might call the welfare department. Leni knew that people's children were sometimes taken away from them by city agencies. Briefly she saw again the woman's anxious loving face as she had walked with her youngsters that Sunday.

So what was there to do? Leni felt she could not stand the din very much longer. Here am I, she thought, a white woman and childless. I could find an apartment somewhere else more easily than she could. Yet that would probably be no solution since the next person who moved into my place would have as much objection to the noise as I do. This is how we hurt each other, not meaning to, all of us crowded in here together. The man who lived in the apartment above the family, Franklin, who was himself Black and who lived with his girlfriend and his mother, had already told Leni, when they met on the stairs one day, that the shouts and music came up through his floor, keeping him awake at night, annoying him in the evenings. And it is

only because she has to earn a living and must work at night,
Leni thought, that the children are alone.

The solution, it seemed, was for someone to be there with
them while the mother was gone, but a scrubwoman's salary
would not allow for the hiring of a babysitter. Then why not
you? Leni asked herself. And she knew, even if the mother
would have wanted this or agreed to it, there was no way she,
Leni, would take on that responsibility. She understood the
cruelty of this: that she might work politically for welfare rights
or daycare centers, and in the women's movement she might dem-
onstrate her "support" of all women, but when it came to the situation next door, in this case where the need was so clear, Leni
did not choose to give up her own freedom, her own privilege,
to help this "sister." She wondered whether her worry and concern could have any value at all if she was unwilling to act directly in this woman's behalf.

Leni got up and paced, as if she could shake off the noise. If
only Gretchen were here, Gretchen with her tough self-interest,
who would say, "You can't take care of other people's children,
Leni. You have rights too. You have the right to a decent environment. Those people are encroaching on your space and you
shouldn't tolerate it!"

Leni heard a crash in the hallway of the apartment next door,
followed by loud frantic crying. She felt sad and disgusted, and
as desperate as the child on the other side of the wall.

* * *

The days went on. Leni worked, drank beer, fretted under
the noise. She wrote to the U.S. Department of State to inquire
about the disappearance of certain Chilean citizens who were
presumably being held in secret political prisons, and, with irony,
she compared her hurt, her loneliness and the inconvenience of
her life with the sufferings of the people of Chile.

Each night she read, sitting propped in the bed in the blue
room. And she remembered how on all those Saturdays when
Gretchen had been decorating the apartment—rearranging furniture, hanging new pictures, bringing in dried weeds to place in a

vase on the mantel—on all those days Leni had sat reading.
When Gretchen asked her help to position a picture, to nail
something in place, Leni got up grudgingly, her mind still engaged with the book. Gretchen had said she did not understand
how Leni could care so little about their home, and Leni had
felt vaguely guilty. Eventually it had become a joke between
them, Gretchen telling their friends how one day burglars might
carry out a chair with Leni in it, reading, not even noticing. She
had invented variations on that theme, and always there was the
ragged edge of resentment beneath her teasing. Now Leni was
alone with her books.

She eagerly awaited each visit with Gretchen. They had no
plans to spend Christmas together: Gretchen had told Leni
she no longer wanted to make plans, that she wanted to live
spontaneously, in a way that was true to herself in each moment.
Then one evening a few days before Christmas, the call came.

"Hi, it's me." Plaintive, almost timid.

Leni felt a rush of pleasure at the sound. My old friend! My
best friend, her whole self responded.

"Hel*lo*. It's so good to hear you!"

A silence. And then, "Leni, I feel so awful. I'm all turned
around, somehow." Gretchen was quiet for a few moments. "I
wrote you a letter today."

Leni waited. She was standing at the phone in the kitchen,
and she looked at the plate and cup stacked in the sink.

"What's wrong?" she asked.

She could hear the sound of Gretchen's crying, and then the
voice came squeaky through the phone.

"I don't know why I'm up here. I miss you so much."

Leni brought the phone to the table and sat down. She stared
at a poster on the wall advertising a women's film festival.
Gretchen's voice was like a small furry animal, wriggling in to
lie warmly against her heart. And yet her mind said angrily, If
you like me so much, why did you leave? And then her mind
said, What's wrong, aren't you getting what you need from
Donna?

"Each day I think about you," Gretchen said, "and I walk in
a room and I wonder, Where is Leni?"

"I'm right here," Leni said, and thought, It's the same for me.
I wonder where *you* are. And she felt tears press at her eyelids.

"Do you have plans for Christmas?" Gretchen asked, and before Leni could answer, she went on, "Will you come up here on
the bus tomorrow, please? There's a good film showing in town,
and then the next day we could have Christmas together. We
can have a fire in the fireplace, and we'll take a walk in the
woods. I need to see you."

When Leni put down the phone she stood for a long time in
the kitchen, letting her reactions wash through her. Perhaps she
should have said, Sorry you're having a tough time, too bad I
already have plans. But she had no heart for such refusals. She
was simply glad and grateful that Gretchen wanted to see her.

On Christmas day, Leni wrote in her journal:

> I arrived on the bus and we were so happy to see each other.
> What a joy! It felt like our first year together, when Gretchen
> was working down in San Jose and I'd ride the bus down to see
> her, and I'd be so excited all the way.
>
> We came back to the country house that's all prettied up now,
> the way she always does with a house, and we made love right
> away, couldn't wait till after dinner. Then we ate and went into
> Guerneville to the movie house to see "Tales of Beatrix Potter,"
> the movie done by the Royal Ballet, that I love so much. Came
> home, drank brandy, talked, slept.
>
> But this morning the grief came on. All of a sudden it was
> all there, Gretchen rejecting me these last few months, how that
> feels, and she feeling terrible because of what she'd put me
> through. She said when she drove out of the city on Wednesday
> she finally realized that she risked losing me. She talked with
> Donna about it that night but couldn't make it better. Then,
> up here alone the next day, she really went through it, just
> feeling how much she does care for me and how much we have
> together. She's been trying to get away from that during the
> whole move, but here she was alone in the country house, in the
> cold and dark, really alone.
>
> So this morning we cried a lot, both of us, letting out the
> grief. And then she realized she was crying not for just now
> but for the whole last year when we'd been so distant from each
> other, and how she needed so much and hadn't been able to ask
> me. That's her pride, I guess, the way she's always been—tough

and proud. But I know too that when she did try to ask me I
didn't hear her, I was so involved in my own problems.
     She says she misses me a lot already.

They walked on a path in woods thick with greenish light, the
ground wet and spongy with pine needles, the air dense with the
smell of trees and rot. Leni walked next to Gretchen, and her
body opened to take in the dampness and the heady smells.
Gretchen's face, shaded by the floppy brim of her black hat,
turned to Leni, her dark eyes loving, and Leni thought she
looked beautiful with her thick hair curling behind her ears, her
face relaxed. Leni had to admit to herself that this living in the
country seemed the right thing for Gretchen.
     Back at the house, they made a safe warm place for each other,
so familiar—making a home for each other as they had done for
four years now—as they built a fire and sat before it to eat their
dinner. They held each other and made love once again, ravished
by tenderness. And when they went upstairs to bed, later, they
screeched at the coldness of the flannel sheets, curled together as
they warmed, and fell into a deep and satisfied sleep.

                              * * *

Five years before, Leni and Gretchen had met in a bar, both
of them having just ended a long relationship. Leni had liked
Gretchen's wit and energy, her air of knowing how to get along
in the world. Gretchen had just started working as a carpenter,
and she was excited about learning a trade, pleased with herself.
She had been drawn to Leni's thoughtfulness, her gentleness,
and a certain large patience that made her seem safe and steady.
They circled around each other for a time, never quite getting
together as each was busy having casual, safe sexual relationships
with other women; perhaps they avoided each other because
they sensed the strength of feeling possible between them and
were not ready to plunge again into something so serious. When
finally they spent a night and morning together, in their lovemaking, their talking, holding each other, they went to a place
of absolute stillness in themselves; and there was no question of
being ready, of needing time, of holding back to protect them-

selves. They felt a great wash of relief, a peacefulness that had
not been possible with any of the other lovers. And from this
arose a tremendous enthusiasm for each other. Very soon they
were spending all their spare time together, and everything they
did was an adventure: they went to the first women's music festival and took off their clothes in the sun with hundreds of other
lesbians, Gretchen shocked and delighted at the sight of so many
nude women; Leni introduced Gretchen to her political friends;
they passed out leaflets at demonstrations, hiked in the woods,
danced until the bars closed, drove to the ocean at dawn.

Leni found Gretchen always affectionate and responsive, and
Gretchen took care of Leni in ways that made her feel secure.
After a year, they decided to find an apartment together, and
once they were settled, there was another kind of joy: the intimacy, the deep commitment and awareness of each other that
was expressed in the least of actions. Gretchen decorated the
apartment; she hung the posters and positioned the plants, put
up the shelves. And they settled in to a life that, despite Gretch-
en's moods and her quick anger, was consistently pleasing.

But in the last year much had changed. Up until eight months
ago, Leni worked as a secretary in one of the finance firms down
on Montgomery Street. There she helped organize a push for
better pay and working conditions for the women. The battle
was lost, and her employers managed to fire her in such a way
that she could not draw unemployment. Leni sank into a depression; she stayed home, letting Gretchen pay the rent and
buy the food, and feeling guilty about that. And Gretchen began to talk about trying to get money together to buy a house,
about getting away from their neighborhood, their alley caught
between the elevated curve of freeway and the stark two-block-
long prisonlike structure of housing project. Leni, resentful and
discouraged, would not hear of moving. She had stopped listening to Gretchen during the long nasty battle at her job. During
those months she was completely obsessed with that struggle.
There were no adventures, no fun, only Leni talking night after
night about the situation at work, Gretchen retreating finally to
sit before the television set. Then, after she lost her job, Leni sat

depressed in the middle room, came silent and distracted to meals, while Gretchen tried to talk with her. Only recently did Leni go out to take short jobs through a temporary secretarial agency, to support herself once again. It had been a hard year for them both, and Leni thought perhaps they were lucky to be able to spend this Christmas so intimately together. Perhaps Gretchen had done the right thing after all in arranging to live separately in this little cabin, take time for herself, find out what she needed.

Their only fight during that weekend came when Gretchen told Leni that she had another lover now besides Donna. This new woman, Polly, whom Leni knew also, had taken to driving up from Berkeley to visit Gretchen. Polly worked as an installer for the telephone company. She had tremendous energy, a strong enthusiasm for living that Gretchen liked. "She said she'd been interested in me for a long time and wanted to get to know me better," Gretchen explained to Leni's stony face.

Leni said a number of derogatory things about Polly, and went on to accuse Gretchen of seducing everyone who walked in her door.

Gretchen flared. "You have no right to make a judgment on me! I like Polly. I like sleeping with her. There's nothing wrong with it and I intend to continue."

"Looks like you're gonna keep yourself pretty busy up here," Leni said in a heavily sarcastic voice. "There's Donna, there's Polly, there's me. Who's next?"

Gretchen stared at her, her dark eyes hard.

Leni went off to sit by herself, and later she told Gretchen shakily, "It makes me feel that you don't care about *me*."

Gretchen took her hand. "Oh no, you're *special* to me, no matter who else I'm sleeping with. Our relationship is much more important than the others."

Leni believed her, for the moment, but still the knowledge of Gretchen's intimacy with two other women now was a discomfort in Leni's chest, something that made her turn and look behind her, anxiously.

* * *

When Leni came back to the city, alone, the alley seemed especially grim. She had always thought the grey shingles of their building were ugly, but now the place seemed grimy and desolate. She opened the gate and came into the entranceway, looking up to see Franklin bounce down the stairs toward her. Franklin was a tall muscular man whose molasses-brown skin gleamed with highlights. He grinned at Leni.

"Hey, how you doin? Been on a trip?"

Leni nodded, setting her small suitcase down before her door.

Franklin turned to frown at the noise spilling out the broken window of the door next to hers.

"Now that's enough to send anybody out of town."

"Was it any better this weekend?" Leni asked.

"Naw, it comes up right through the floor. I talked to that woman, but she doesn't do a thing about those kids."

He went past Leni and paused, holding open the gate, looking back at her.

"I finally called Chiu last night. He didn't even know there were kids *living* there. Said two people rented it as a childless couple. He's gonna come over and see for himself soon as he can get to it."

"That's too bad."

"Damn right. You take care now." And Franklin stepped outside the gate, pushed it closed to latch, and was gone.

Leni stood looking at her own door. The peace, the expansiveness she had felt in the country left her. So Franklin had called Mr. Chiu. That was like him. He was a man wound up very tight. He worked long hours running a quick-printing business, kept a gun in his apartment, and held a black belt in karate which he maintained by training regularly. No one, not even his mother, called him Frank. Given the opportunity, he would lecture in a quick bitter voice about the corruption of police and city officials; he deplored the high crime rate. He was ready to kill anyone who messed with him, and had the means to do so. He was always briskly friendly to Leni. She knew that he was aware that she and Gretchen were lesbians, but this did not seem to affect his behavior toward them. Franklin was almost a friend. But Leni thought of him as dangerous, like a bomb that could go off one day, devastating everything in sight.

As she went in her apartment, it seemed shadowy and dank to her. Several of the rooms were almost empty now, with Gretchen's things gone. They seemed forlorn.

Deliberately, Leni gathered the memories from the weekend with Gretchen and held them close to her. Gretchen loved her. They were still lovers, delighting in each other physically; they were still loyal and caring. Perhaps that could sustain her.

When she sat in bed reading, later, she began to feel satisfied, here. The noise from next door had quieted somewhat. The bed was warm, and the cat lay curled in her lap. She had been reading Seth, *The Nature of Personal Reality*, and stopping to think after each paragraph, to assess the ideas and apply them to her own experience. Suddenly, in surprise, she realized she was glad to be alone. Gretchen had always fussed about at night, tucking and plumping, and she could read in bed for only a few minutes before the book dropped out of her hands and her eyes closed. Then Leni had felt guilty for keeping the light on, and had closed the book before she wanted to, to turn out the light and lie next to Gretchen in the dark.

That night very late, she put down the book and took her notebook from the bed table, to write:

> Seeing the possibilities in solitude.
>
> When your lover's here, there's some way that limits how far you can go with your thoughts. Like, if she isn't interested in this or that, I can't really get into it myself.
>
> If you're alone, your mind can just follow it's own direction out into a subject, just follow the natural curve of interest.

But in the morning she awoke in the pale silent dawn to the memory of the last time she and Gretchen had made love in this bed. In early December Leni had persuaded Gretchen to go with her to a counselor, although both of them were worried about the money it would cost. There Leni had surprised herself by admitting that she had wanted to push Gretchen away, and with a rush of shame and relief she had said, "I couldn't stand her loving me so much. I despised her for it. How could she love me so much when I had failed, when I didn't deserve it!"

In the car afterwards, she had cried, and Gretchen held her. They went home and ate and that night made love very tenderly at first, Leni experiencing a powerful possessiveness of Gretchen's body, the dark curling pubic hair, the short back and flat buttocks. She suffered momentary excruciating visions of Donna touching Gretchen's thighs, fondling her shoulders, and she wanted to make love to Gretchen more passionately, more sensitively than Donna possibly could. Light from the city penetrated dimly through the yellow drape at the window. "I want to see you better," Leni said, and she went to Gretchen's altar to bring back a candle, light it and put it next to the bed. Then she touched Gretchen slowly, gently, as she knew Gretchen preferred, spending minutes stroking her shoulders, cupping her breast and coming near the nipple but not quite touching it yet. She watched the expressions cross Gretchen's face like ripples on water, one changing to another: absorption, surprise, longing. Gretchen's hands caressed her belly and thighs as she slid her finger between Gretchen's buttocks and carefully massaged the tight little mouth of anus. When she slipped her finger inside, Gretchen gave a soft moan. Leni felt her own cunt throbbing as she leaned at last to take Gretchen's nipple in her mouth. When finally she moved down Gretchen's body, kissing, sucking, Gretchen writhed, clinging to her shoulders, lifting her hips and opening her legs to receive Leni's mouth. Leni touched lightly with her tongue, circling the tight nub of clitoris, stroking the insides of the lips. She slipped two fingers into Gretchen's wet vagina and moved them subtly. Her lovemaking was lengthy and inspired, until Gretchen whispered, "Come up here, Leni, I want to suck you too." She turned around then, lay against Gretchen's body, offered her own vulva to Gretchen's mouth as she closed her lips over Gretchen's clitoris, moving insistently now, her motion quickened by the delirium aroused by Gretchen's mouth on her, until Gretchen called out first, then Leni, caught up in a rousing, rending climax.

Finally, when they had lain back, could look in each other's faces, Gretchen's body had been open to Leni in the old way, her eyes dark pools ready to swallow Leni. Leni remembered exulting, *Now I have her again. She's mine.* And the memory was a pain down the front of her body now as she lay alone in this same bed.

* * *

The next weekend when Leni went up to visit Gretchen, she found her distressed, feeling overwhelmed and scared of being in the country alone, afraid she would not be able to get enough carpentry jobs to support herself, afraid she would be completely isolated, afraid that Leni was judging her for what she had done.

Leni spent the weekend taking care of Gretchen. She helped her make little signs offering her carpentry skills, and took her to the stores and coffee shops in the area to hang them up; she went with Gretchen to meet her neighbors in the house next door; she stood by while Gretchen called the one lesbian they knew up there and made a date for dinner with her. She cooked for Gretchen, held her a lot, and on the way to the bus, bouncing along in the big station wagon, she gave Gretchen a peptalk, as they had done for each other so many times, just like Mickey Rooney in the movies telling Judy Garland before the big opening night: "You can do it, kid. Get in there and show 'em!"

As they hugged at the bus stop in Santa Rosa, Gretchen said, "Thank you, honey. You're so good to me." And she stepped back to clasp Leni's shoulders and look admiringly at her.

The bus rolled down Route 101 toward San Francisco, and Leni stared out the window, feeling drained. All weekend her mind and emotions had been focused on Gretchen; she had not even been able to relax enough to enjoy the trees, the fresh fragrant air. While she was giving it, she had not begrudged Gretchen the attention, but now she was tired, and she wished, in retrospect, that there had been some time given to *her,* some few moments when Gretchen had listened to *her.*

It was the appropriate beginning to a nightmarish week. At work Leni's boss had redesigned all the forms they used and had changed the procedures to conform to a new computerized process. These changes, which Leni did not consider improvements, required relearning all the fundamentals of her job. She came home each evening exhausted and throbbing with tension. And each night, lying in her bed, she suffered under the constant noise from next door, sometimes so loud she could not even concentrate to read. Many times during the night she awoke to stare upward in the dark, tense with panic, imagining a burglar or rapist in her room, until she recognized the familiar thumps and shouts through the wall.

Gretchen was to arrive on Saturday morning. Leni eagerly awaited her coming, and yet she found herself angry at Gretchen, with a resentment that grew more intense every day. The next Tuesday she wrote in her notebook:

> By the time Gretchen arrived on Saturday I was really in a funk, and just so mad at her, all of it spewing out of me. Seemed like it was her fault that I'm having to go through all these changes and having to deal with all this stuff here. So I was letting her have it, how pissed I am at her, and she just listened, and then she said she's sorry I'm having a hard time, she's really sorry, and I started to cry. Once I was crying I couldn't stop, and she just put her arms around me and rocked me.
>
> You know when you live alone there's no one to do that for you. You've got to be a grown-up all the time. When she lived here with me we did that a lot for each other, just comforted each other, or listened or joked to make each other feel better.
>
> The weekend was okay but Monday morning was the pits again, so Gretchen said she'd stay around and do some things she had to do and help me ease out in the evening when I came home from work. I was feeling relieved, loving Gretchen a lot. When I got home, we ate and went to sleep early, feeling really close.

At 2:00 a.m. that night the doorbell sounded in a loud jangling through the apartment. Gretchen dragged herself up out of bed to answer it, and Leni came behind her, pulling on a bathrobe. There outside the door stood a skinny barefooted little boy in pajamas, his shoulders hunched tightly forward, his breath coming in loud gasps. Leni and Gretchen stood looking down at him, sleepy and not understanding what was happening.

He rasped out a word, and Leni bent to catch it. "What? What?" He spoke again and she made out "Asth . . . ma . . . ."

Gretchen reached to support him as he swayed. She led him into the living room to ease him into a chair.

"Should I call an ambulance?" Leni asked, and watched the boy's head bob in agreement.

Gretchen stooped next to the child, rubbing his back. "Where's your mother?" she asked.

He fought for breath, managed to say, "At. . .work."

"Why didn't your older sister help you?!" Leni asked him.

Again that hollow, strained, old man's voice. "She. . .wouldn't wake up."

And then he leaned forward out of Gretchen's arms and vomited on the floor.

Gretchen glanced up at Leni. "You better call an ambulance, and go next door to get his sister."

In the next twenty minutes they roused the sister, who came to their door with white plastic curlers in her hair, looking scared and bewildered; they phoned for an ambulance, and tried to make the boy more comfortable, as the front room filled with the sounds of his struggle to breathe. They stood around him, waiting.

"Is there some way we can reach your mother?" Leni asked the sister.

She shook her head. "She at work."

"But is there a phone there? Could we call her?"

The girl gazed blankly at Leni.

Then the ambulance attendants arrived, seeming very large and official in their uniforms. "Anyone to go with him?" one of them asked as the other picked up the boy and headed out the door.

"This is his sister here," Leni said.

"Okay, let's go."

She watched the young girl trail out after the man and get into the ambulance with her brother. Then Leni shut the door. Gretchen had gone to the kitchen for paper towels and was mopping up the vomit.

"You'd think his mother would have arranged something," Gretchen muttered.

"I don't know, I don't know."

And then they sat next to each other on the bed, equally worried, similarly brought down by the incident.

That morning Gretchen left in her station wagon to drive up to the country again. Leni waved from the window, then turned quickly and came back down the hall to get ready for work. She was tired, and filled with sadness.

But it was not until several days later that this sorrow was released. Leni had come home early from work to find the two oldest girls from next door going in the gate. As she followed them, she saw the landlord standing at the doorway talking to their mother. Mr. Chiu was a stocky Chinese man with straight thin hair brushed down at the sides of his head. He had always been a friendly and responsible landlord. Now he shifted uncomfortably before the door, his face tense.

The two girls, bright eyed and innocent, both said "Hi," to Leni, just as she heard Mr. Chiu saying, "If you get out tomorrow, I repay you on the rent. You tell me when you going and I pay you back the difference . . . okay?"

The woman stood inside the doorway staring at him. Her face was slack, her eyes stricken.

"You do that, I pay you back for rest of month. You leave this week, okay?"

Slowly she nodded, saying yes, yes in a barely audible voice. As Leni came past them, the woman's eyes met hers for one instant in a desperate, accusing glance.

Leni went inside and closed her door behind her. In the bedroom she sat down on the bed and leaned over, her arms around her middle, staring at the floor. Then she bent farther, resting her head on her knees.

She cried, for the woman, for the cheerful, unknowing little girls, for the boy struggling to breathe. And their dilemma pushed her more deeply inside herself, to that place she knew well, from which absolutely nothing mattered. It was like being locked in a dungeon. Caught there, Leni couldn't move, and even when the cat crawled up on her back and settled itself between her shoulder blades, she did not stir. It was only much later, when the bedroom was thick with darkness, that a small voice spoke in Leni's mind, saying, You are getting into a bad state, Leni. You'd better *do* something about yourself. And Leni pondered that center of herself that was inert, was ultimately yielding. Her political activity, her working at jobs, both made her look as if she were really active in her own behalf. But Leni knew that at this center where only she could act, could *take care* of herself, she had abdicated long ago. Not all women did that, she knew, but she had done it, as an adolescent. She had given in to her father, whom she loved, had pulled back her power, stepped away from her own necessities, had sat passive within the muddle of her personality and found other people to take care of her. For half of her life she had been this way.

Gradually, stiffly, Leni raised herself to sit upright on the bed and looked down at her knees. She was filled with repulsion, and a voice different from the first one spoke in her, saying, You might as well be dead.

Frightened, Leni shook her head.

What do you want now? asked the voice. Do you want to eat dinner? Do you want to kill yourself? Do you want to take a bath?

For a few moments Leni sat contemplating the choices, finding them equal, and then with a great wrenching effort she stood up from the bed and went to the hallway. Here she walked back and forth from kitchen to front door, and the first voice repeated quietly, . . . better *do* something, Leni. . . .

* * *

For days then Leni moved in a strange, detached way through her life, going to work, coming home. She didn't drink beer or read her beloved books: she sat in a chair in the living room and stared at the plants. She felt totally sane, perfectly lucid and aware of everything around her, and there before her was a picture of herself, a woman who had never in her life made an active choice, who had given in to other people's desires, lived out their aspirations. Some part of her knew how extreme this vision

was—she had done many things in her life, hadn't she?—but no
matter how bizarre or one-sided it was, it stood before her with
undeniable authority now, and it controlled her.

She called a friend to try to talk about this, and the friend did
not understand her. Finally, after many more days, Leni called
Gretchen one night. She could feel Gretchen listening intently,
and when she was finished, Gretchen asked her a few questions;
Leni recognized that Gretchen was worried for her. And then
Gretchen suggested she go to one of the week-long country retreats led by Alicia Brown, that practical young woman whom
Leni had liked when Gretchen had taken her to Alicia's meditation group.

"I can't see myself doing that," Leni said. "I mean, one night
was okay, but a *whole week*!? That seems really self-indulgent."

"You need to take care of yourself, Leni," Gretchen coun-
tered. "You've started already, I know, reading Seth, so why
not take this opportunity to go ahead and do some intensive
work on yourself?"

"Well, reading Seth is one thing, but . . ." And Leni did not
say that a further cause of her aversion was the fact that it had
been at one such retreat that Gretchen had become lovers with
Donna.

Gretchen talked quietly, describing the atmosphere of support at the retreat, telling Leni about the exercises. "It's healing," she said. "It's a safe place to get yourself together." Her
examples made the experience seem simple and wholesome, no
more bizarre than those few meditation group meetings Leni
had attended.

After they had talked for a half hour or so, Leni was finally
persuaded that being in the country with a group of women, di-
recting attention to herself, could possibly lead her to make
some decision concerning her life. She had realized, recently,
that she lived in a state of perpetual waiting for Gretchen to
come back home. And as soon as she realized this, she hated it,
for it made her horribly dependent.

That very week she was reminded of how vulnerable she was
when she discovered that Gretchen had become lovers with
Chandra, the country woman Leni had urged her to seek out.

Gretchen told Leni about this on the phone, and elaborated, "I feel like in my life right now I need to learn through having relationships. That's where the emphasis needs to be right now. I know it." Leni said nothing, but when she had put down the phone she paced the apartment, raging at Gretchen, and she knew more than ever that she had to get away, to *change* something.

The retreat was to begin in a few days. Leni found someone to feed her cat, and she arranged to ride up to Petaluma with some women from Berkeley. Then on Friday she went in to the temporary agency that had placed her in her present job and told them her mother was very ill, she had to go to New Jersey, and she thought she could be back in a week. They told her they would have to place someone else in her job, but probably they could get her another one as soon as she returned. Leni thanked them. She packed the few clothes suggested in the pamphlet describing the retreat, made sure she had her notebook and pen and the colored pencils specified. And then she panicked. How could she be with people just now, feeling as she did about herself! It did not seem possible. She spent a dreadful two days, hidden away in her apartment, and when the women came to pick her up, she stood staring out through the gate, her stomach tight with fear. In the car with them, she tried at first to act her former cordial self, but finally gave up and fell silent, sure that they were judging her, that they thought her strange and inadequate.

The retreat was held at a private home in the rolling yellow hills outside Petaluma. A creek ran through the property, and a few sheep grazed behind a wire fence. There was a long low house nestled among trees; a barn with a woodstove in the large room below, and sleeping rooms above. Other small structures— a cabin, the frame of a geodesic dome, a teepee—were scattered on several acres of land. When Leni arrived, her senses awoke to the smell of grass, the sound of the stream tumbling over a rocky bed, the calls of birds.

There were thirty-five participants gathered, and four facilitators led by Alicia Brown. Leni found herself private and forlorn among so many women. She knew only a few of them, and was

so shaky at first that she did not dare introduce herself to any of
the others. Soon it did not seem to matter much as they plunged
into a grueling schedule of sessions in which one or the other of
the facilitators led them in exercises designed to confront them
with the problems in their lives and suggest solutions.

To her dismay, Leni began to re-experience her disillusion-
ment over her job last year. Once again she felt the idealism
with which she had joined the struggle at that office. She and a
few other women had truly believed when they began that the
managers would see the justice of their demands and grant them
the benefits the women so sorely needed for themselves and
their families. But as the weeks passed and there was no response to their requests, they realized how naive they had been.
Then when they tried to get all the women together to work out
a different plan, they were thwarted at every turn. If they hung
up leaflets, the personnel director sent his assistant to tear them
down; if they talked to people personally, the supervisors threat-
ened the women, saying, "It wouldn't be wise for you to go to
that meeting," or gave them extra work to do on their lunch
hours so they could not attend. Still some women joined them,
and the conflict accelerated. Leni learned how determined man-
agement was to stamp out any attempt by the secretaries to organize themselves, and she saw how much power the managers
wielded. Eventually most of the women, out of fear of losing
their jobs, or out of weariness, or because they could not stand
the harrassment, stopped coming to the meetings and would not
listen to Leni and her few compatriots anymore. Leni understood their caution, for they had children, families to support,
but she was despairing and she blamed herself: she had not
found the way to communicate to them her absolute conviction
that if all stood together they could not be defeated. When she
was fired, she knew how miserably she had failed, for her dis-
missal was a lesson to the other women, an act designed to make
them even more frightened and subservient.

Here at the retreat, Leni examined this experience, and in the
sessions she was encouraged to ask herself what could have been
done differently, to reconstruct the circumstances in a number

of alternate ways. It was suggested that she had done all she could given the knowledge she had at the time, and that the failure had been the result not of some lack in herself or in the other women but because of the obstacles in the situation itself. Alicia Brown urged Leni to appreciate the effort and dedication of herself and the other women, to forgive herself for the mistakes she had made, and to be truly open to receive the wealth of learning available to her from that series of events. Leni couldn't do it. It seemed too pat and easy a glossing over of the real experience of all those human beings. But as they worked on this she did feel in herself the beginning of a different way to view the matter, the most fragile new inklings of acceptance of herself in that situation. Finally she became impatient with this old pain, was ready to let it sink away from her, wanting to leave it behind for now.

In the sessions she began to ask herself what she wanted, and by the third day she understood she had three desires: to move from the apartment in the alley to a cheaper place which would be pleasant and safe; to do some kind of work other than secretarial; to entertain the idea of having a lover besides Gretchen. By far the most difficult of these was the first. She spelled out what she would get from the move: pay less rent, freedom from fear, a sense of calm and harmony. But when she was asked to consider what she would have to give up, she knew she was not ready, and she wrote in her notebook,

> Hard to admit that for a long time I've gotten off on the idea of myself as a victim, living in that apartment in the ghetto, feeling real self-righteous about living in the slums. And the drunks and the addicts and the bums on the street, and the beaten tired people. Being around them keeps me in touch with the hard lives that most people have to live. It connects me up to humanity, or that's how I see it. Guess I'm not ready to leave that behind.
>
> And then too, in that apartment are all the memories of the life Gretchen and I lived there. All those days and weeks and years, so dear to me.
>
> I'm not ready to choose to move yet. I'll just have to think about it more. Really, the move would mean taking control of my life. It would mean trusting in my own strength.

These realizations plunged Leni inside herself where she suffered acutely. That evening, as the group of women sat in a circle in the main room of the house, she wished so much to be
comforted.

In the evening ritual a Hopi Indian rattle was passed from
hand to hand, and the woman who held the rattle could speak
uninterrupted, could sing or recite or do whatever would express
what she needed to communicate to the others.

Now the woman with the rattle said, "Last night in the barn
I was sitting alone, and I started to cry." Leni looked up in surprise. "I haven't cried in a year," the woman continued. "I
don't know what's happening to me."

The rattle was passed, until another woman said, "I have been
grieving. I feel myself grieving and I can't hold it in anymore."

This was a woman who had seemed cheerful and confident in
the previous days. Leni hadn't imagined she could have been
sad.

Then as Leni held the rattle and shook it, she was stopped by
some of the faces in the circle, impatient or bored, but she met
the eyes of the two women who had spoken, and she took a
deep breath. "I don't know why but I am filled up with sorrow," she said. "There's a pain in me. I want your help with it."

She sat in silence for a time, looking around her. No one
moved or spoke. Leni felt as if she were strapped tightly around
her chest, air thick against her temples.

A woman named Adrian, next to her, took the rattle and
leaned forward to look at Leni. "I'm *glad* you said you're feeling bad!"

Leni heard herself give a harsh, surprised laugh.

Adrian lifted a hand. "No, no, I don't mean I'm glad you're
feeling bad, but that you expressed it. I think a lot of people've
been feeling it but there's been no way to let it out."

Leni was retreating into some dark constricted place. She
looked at her hands gripped over her crossed ankles, as the rattle
passed on around the circle—to women who spoke of other
things: the schedule for tonight, arrangements for lunch tomorrow. Her head lowered.

Then she heard the voice of a woman named Windstone. Leni
had met Windstone several times, but the name had put her off,
so that she had not bothered to get to know her. It was hard for
Leni to accept these women who called themselves Willow or
Comfrey or Moonwoman, these New Age dykes who lived in
country places and conducted their lives by consulting astrology
books or the *I Ching,* who knew more about ancient herbal rem-
edies than they did about what was going on in the world right
now. They inhabited such a different mental realm from Leni's
that she did not know how to communicate with them.

But at this moment Windstone was talking, and Leni turned
to look along the line of faces to those bright eyes watching her
from the side. Windstone shook the rattle, its feathers bobbing,
and said loudly, "I would like to be *held* by about ten people!"

Leni saw then not Windstone's name or lifestyle but only the
need she had spoken, and before she could think or honor her
reservations she was up on her knees and crawling toward Windstone. Other women reached her at the same moment as Leni,
and they fell into each others' bodies, Windstone and Leni on
the bottom, arms, legs, shoulders, hips cradling them. Leni's
face was pressed into Windstone's chest. Someone's arm circled
them tightly. Someone was moaning, and Leni found herself
asking brokenly, "How will I live without it? How will I live
without it?"

A voice close against her back answered, "You will. Something in *you* will take its place."

That evening, Leni slept outside, gazing up at the distant stars,
and she felt very still and grateful.

In the last two days of the retreat, she found herself often
with Windstone, and was not displeased by that. Windstone was
a decade younger than Leni; instead of getting married, as Leni
had done at age twenty, Windstone had gone off to the woods
of Oregon to live with other lesbians and discover what the idea
of women's strength and community might mean. She was a
big woman with long legs and broad shoulders, creamy skin and
clear hazel eyes of riveting brightness. Now she lived in Oakland
and was studying massage and various forms of "bodywork"—a

word Leni did not understand, except as it meant the hammering out of car fenders.

Leni wrote in her notebook:

> I went down to the barn to build a fire in the stove, which was
> my chore for the evening, and there was Windstone sitting in the
> shadows playing her flute. And I saw she had already started the
> fire, so I turned around to leave, cause it seemed like she wanted
> to be alone. But she asked me to stay. So I began stoking the fire,
> and she went on playing her flute for a while. Then she came to
> sit next to me and we talked, and pretty soon we were talking
> about what it takes to keep going, about perseverance, about
> work, about how sometimes you have to keep on going farther
> than you think you're able. And then she told me I was helping
> her, that she had been feeling like her work was worthless and she
> ought to just give it up, but talking with me had centered her again,
> and made her feel like she was back inside herself.
>
> So then after I left her to come back up to the house, I was
> feeling really calm and just open to myself and everybody else,
> peaceful.

The next night Windstone asked to sleep near Leni. They
went back late to the barn and spread out their sleeping bags in
the straw of the main room. Once there, Windstone put her arm
around Leni and hugged her. Leni felt the smooth skin of her
cheek, breathed in her warm clean smell.

"There's something I want to talk to you about," Windstone
whispered.

"Yes?" Leni whispered back.

"Well, this is awkward, but . . . well, I'm attracted to you, but
there's something I want to check out first. I mean I met Gretch-
en up here with some other people, and I know the two of you
are having problems and I don't want to get caught in the middle
or get used . . . ."

Leni rolled away from her, snorting in disgust. "You've just
succeeded in making me unhappy."

"What do you mean?"

A chorus of hisses from the darkness told them they were
talking too loud.

"The last person I want to think about right now is *Gretchen*," Leni whispered. She could make out Windstone's big clear eyes staring at her through the dimness. "Look," she said, "you don't have to worry about coming between her and me. I hope this won't insult you, but you're just not someone I could fall in love with."

"Oh?" Windstone looked both hurt and intrigued. "Why not?"

Leni propped herself on her elbows in the straw, pulling the sleeping bag up over her shoulders.

"First of all, you're ten years younger than me. You're a whole other generation of women. I doubt that you could understand much about my life. Then too, you're a masseuse or something, and I'm a secretary, which is a very different mindset. You're spiritual and I'm political, which is also pretty far apart. *And* someone told me, too, that you've got lovers all over the place. I'd be *crazy* to take you seriously!"

Windstone smiled, relieved, as if she would say, Oh, is *that* all."

"There's something between us," she said instead. "It's a strong connection. The other night when we talked here in the barn I began to understand how you're important to me."

"Oh really?" Leni was getting very tired, wishing they could go to sleep.

"I don't mean to talk it to death," Windstone whispered.

"No," Leni said sleepily, and she closed her eyes.

Then she felt a hand on her cheek, and lips touching hers in a light kiss. A voice spoke close to her ear. "Goodnight Leni."

Leni found that she was powerfully attracted to Windstone, but she knew by now that attraction did not have to be acted on, or if it *were* acted on, it didn't have to be given any particular importance. The truth was that she had begun to miss Gretchen, to long to share her new insights with her. So that the next night when Windstone took her hand and led her back through the darkness to the barn, to a little room with a bed in it, Leni followed willingly, thinking yes I'll do this and it'll only be what it is, surely no more important to me or Windstone than any of her other involvements. This cynicism made her comfortable, so that while Windstone lit a candle, Leni took off her clothes and waited. Windstone slipped out of her clothes and turned to Leni. On her throat was a delicate silver necklace, the figure of a winged woman, that caught the warm candle light and held it. Her body looked strong, with high round breasts and wide shoulders. It welcomed Leni. An expanse of body, holding her. A body like bread. It felt wonderful as they lay on the bed stroking each other, as they began to make love.

Nevertheless, the next day Leni spoke with Gretchen on the phone and learned she would be at their San Francisco apartment when Leni came home. In her pleasure at this news, she put aside the attraction for Windstone, filed the lovemaking away as a one-night stand, and prepared to return to the city.

But Windstone caught her on the porch of the house as everyone was cleaning up on the last morning.

"Will you come with us to the restaurant in Santa Rosa for lunch?"

"No, I want to go home."

"I'd really like you to come."

"No."

"Then when will we see each other again?"

Discomfort. How to explain this to Gretchen. How to make a date with Windstone without hurting Gretchen.

"Friday night?" Windstone asked.

"Uhm . . . I guess so."

"I'll call you Thursday. Okay?"

"Yes."

And then Leni was riding in the back seat of a car down Route 101 to San Francisco, and she was thinking that now she knew so much more about Gretchen's experience at the retreat in September, and was anticipating their talking together about it. When she got to the apartment, she saw Gretchen's flop-brimmed hat on the kitchen table, and a note saying Gretchen had gone to the therapist and would be back soon.

Leni went into the bedroom and stretched out on the bed to wait. She thought through the week, and felt the changes in herself that had come about at the retreat. In the exercises and meditations she had encountered certain strengths in herself, and certain imperatives, that could not now be ignored. And was there more resolve? More sureness?

Certainly it seemed a little strange to be back in this room, looking at the hanging plants, hearing those familiar noises through the wall. Leni realized that she would probably need a few days to get used to ordinary life again: they had been living such a heightened existence at the retreat.

Soon she heard the sound of the gate slamming, and the turning of Gretchen's key in the door. Her heart jumped in anticipation.

PART II

Everything Changes

Gretchen stood at the foot of the bed. In her plaid shirt and jeans and big country clodhoppers, she stood as if rooted, her shoulders pulled forward, her hands balled into fists at her sides. Leni felt a quick flutter of fear.

"How was the session with Sonya?"

"Good." The word dropped like a stone to the floor.

Gretchen's skin had gone pasty, giving her the look of someone who is about to faint, and her nose stood out sharply from her bloodless cheeks. Leni was familiar with that look. Whenever Gretchen was particularly agitated, the skin would seem to tighten over the curved bone of her nose.

Leni stared at her, wondering what could have happened.

Gretchen's eyes were so bright and pained that they looked feverish.

She said, "Leni, I don't want to be lovers with you anymore."
The breath stopped in Leni's chest.

Gretchen's shoulders hunched determinedly inside her plaid
shirt. "It's been coming on for a while," she said, "and Sonya
helped me admit it."

Behind Gretchen was the foliage of her hanging plants, their
leaves and fronds trembling delicately as she moved now, two
steps to the side, rooted herself again, and looked just past Leni.

"You're too much *in* my life. When I'm with another lover I
keep thinking about what you would think or say about it. I'm
never free of you—your opinions, your demands on me, your
jealousy. I don't want it. I want to be free in my own life."

"But, you . . ." Leni began, her voice rising and breaking.
She rolled sideways in the bed to press the pillow against her
face and felt the mattress lower as Gretchen sat on the corner
farthest away from her.

"It's worse to go on pretending," Gretchen's voice came.

"*Pretending!*" Leni spoke into her pillow.

"We can talk on the phone, keep in touch," Gretchen said.

When finally Leni could look up at Gretchen, she saw her
perched on the corner of the bed, her hands clasped in her lap,
her face tight.

"Do you really mean this?" Leni asked.

Gretchen looked up at her. "Yes. It's what I need."

"Is this forever?"

"I don't know anything like that."

"When will we see each other?"

"I don't know that either."

"Then . . .," Leni's voice came quiet and flat, "you don't
want to see me?"

Gretchen hesitated only a moment, and then said, "No."

Leni rolled over to stare at the ceiling. She was quiet for a
long time, letting this reality settle in her. Then she said, "All
right, I get it."

And then she said, "What are you sitting there for? Hadn't
you better leave? Get on back up into the country? Back to
your life?"

The bed jittered as Gretchen shifted her weight. "I won't leave you right now," she said. "I'll stay the night and leave in the morning."

"I wanted to tell you all about the retreat," Leni said, and began to cry.

After a time Gretchen's voice came. "We can still talk."

Leni turned on her side again, hugging the pillow. "Sure," she muttered. "Sure."

Gretchen did stay the night, but they did not talk. Gretchen went to the kitchen to make some dinner and brought it to Leni in the bedroom, but Leni couldn't eat. She wanted only to sleep. Later Gretchen came to bed and stayed far over on the opposite side from Leni. The few times Leni was awakened in the night by a shout from next door, a crash, she was aware of Gretchen's body tensed away from her.

In the morning Gretchen left early. "I'll call you," she said, and was gone. Leni heard the gate slam.

That afternoon Leni sat on the mattress in the middle room. It was the hour when the sun fell between the buildings into this room, and Leni felt its warmth on her thigh, gratefully. She was drinking strong coffee, having a talk with herself. Now you will have to live differently, she told herself. It's not a shared life anymore. No use waiting. She made it clear. You're on your own. But it was a very wan Mickey Rooney speaking to a dulled-out Judy Garland.

Leni let it go.

There was something else nagging at her, drawing her attention like a motion glimpsed at the corner of one's eye, not quite identifiable, appearing again and again. She went back over the past year remembering the times Gretchen had said to her, "I can't stand living here anymore. I need to be where there's grass and trees"; the times Gretchen had talked to her about buying a house in East Oakland, how lots of dykes were doing it, buying old run-down houses and fixing them up. Gretchen had even contacted a real estate agent and had insisted Leni go with her to look at a few houses. Leni had gone unwillingly. "Oakland and Berkeley are like the suburbs," she had said. "I find the

suburbs depressing." She had not believed they could raise the
money for the down payment; she had not wanted to figure
out how they might swing it. Most of all, she admitted to herself now, she had not taken seriously Gretchen's desire to change
their lives, nor cared about Gretchen's needs. There was something very ugly in this, Leni thought, something so bluntly un-
caring in herself. And the worst part was that in all that time
she had been living on Gretchen's money. She saw it now, what
it really was, when what it had seemed to her was that she had
fought the good fight at work, and lost, and then she had been
so disheartened that she could not think of getting another job.
Gretchen had been sympathetic and supportive, proud of Leni
for her courage. But the bones under that situation were that
for months Gretchen had been paying the rent and buying the
groceries, and when she tried to tell Leni what she needed, when
she asked Leni to help her, Leni paid no attention, or she answered with stubborn sarcasm. Now Leni remembered how,
gradually, Gretchen had sunk away from her; she had begun to
watch television regularly, until when Leni wanted to go out, or
when she wanted to talk about her own problems, Gretchen had
been engaged with the TV set, propped in bed in the darkened
bedroom staring at the screen. It was only when someone
talked her into going to that retreat in September, when she got
involved with Donna, that she came alive again. Leni remembered Gretchen's saying, of Donna, "It's just that she *pays attention* to me. She loves me."

Leni felt sick to her stomach.

* * *

On Thursday, Gretchen called. "How are you?" she asked,
sounding genuinely concerned. And then she tried to explain
herself once again. "Leni, look, if we don't do this separation,
our relationship is screwed, but if we *do* it, well, maybe one day
we can come back together again—as friends, or maybe even
lovers."

We, Leni thought, what d'you mean *we* do this separation.
And when she hung up the phone it was even more clear to her

that Gretchen was truly gone, that she must create a whole new life that did not include Gretchen's actual presence or any expectations about her.

And as if to lay the first stone in that foundation, the phone rang again and Windstone's voice said, "It's Thursday and I said I'd call. Do we have a date for tomorrow night?"

It was six weeks before Leni saw Gretchen again.

* * *

During the first three weeks she cried at least once a day, usually in the morning when she awoke. It embarrassed her that she did it even when she woke up next to Windstone. But Windstone kindly held her while she cried, and soothed her, smoothing the hair back from her forehead, handing her kleenex after kleenex.

Leni did not go back to work at the temporary agency. She called up each of her friends, forcing herself to this action and not mentioning Gretchen unless questioned about her, and she asked each woman if she knew of some work she could do. After five phone calls, the situation seemed grim, but on the sixth Leni talked with Barbara, an old political friend of hers who had become a therapist and was now earning good money. "Did you know I bought a house in Bernal Heights?" Barbara asked. And she told Leni the house was old and needed lots of work, and she didn't know how she would ever accomplish it all. She had so little time. "Want to hire me to work for you?" Leni asked. Barbara hesitated. Leni somehow was certain she could do the work. Her father had been a handyman at home; he had taught her how to hammer a nail and how to saw, and one summer she had helped him remodel the bathroom and build a porch on the back of the house. "I can do it, Barbara. Try me out. We can figure out what to do, together, and then when you have to see clients I can get the job done." Barbara was not quite convinced. "I could only pay you four dollars an hour," she said. Leni did some quick figuring. That would be a little less than five hundred a month. If she were careful, she could live on that. "Where's your house?" she asked. "I'll start tomorrow."

And Leni began a new notebook. This one was not a steno
pad swiped from work but a sidebound book with ruled pages
of pale green paper which she had bought just for herself. She
wanted to start clean, from the moment after Gretchen walked
out, and go on from there.

On February 7, she wrote in the notebook:

> It's 5:45 and the rain's pouring outside. Why is it I can't help
> remembering Gretchen, how we used to wake up each morning,
> how we'd hold each other. Oh shit, I don't want to think about
> this now. Gretchen was my home.
>
> Windstone's getting happy because of me, just how I see her
> and accept her makes her feel good about herself. But I'm not
> happy, and this feels familiar. After I split up with my first
> lover, a lot of the women I related to were made happy by me
> while I was left unsatisfied.
> But maybe now this is happening because it can't be a person
> who satisfies me.
>
> At 7:00 a.m. finally I broke down and called Gretchen. We
> talked, and I was sobbing, and she let me do it. But I felt terrible,
> like I was the weak helpless person and she was the strong one.

The first week of physical labor was difficult for Leni. She
dressed in fatigue pants and workshirt and hiking boots that first
day and took the bus to Bernal Heights where she found the yellow frame house set in a yard behind a picket fence. It looked
shabbily cozy. If I were another person, thought Leni, stepping
up on its porch, I would envy Barbara. Barbara took Leni down
into the basement, where a dirt floor sloped at an extreme angle.
The first task, she explained, was to dig out the floor until it was
level. Then they would have to install concrete piers to hold the
beams they would erect to reinforce the sagging floor of the
kitchen above. Eventually a new concrete basement floor would
be poured. For an hour, Barbara worked next to Leni. Then
she said she had to go upstairs to change clothes and see clients,
and she left Leni alone.

It was hard to dig the shovel down into the packed dirt, to
loosen the damp clods, lift the shovelful of dirt and carry it to

dump at the low end of the basement. Already Leni's back and arms ached, and her legs felt wobbly. But she forced herself to lift the shovel again, push down the blade with her foot, bend to scoop up the dirt. She knew the day would stretch to eternity. To strengthen herself she thought how she might now be sitting at a typewriter doing something as inane as typing labels. This was better, no matter what it cost her. This work made her feel rough, like a bear, like a tough dyke, and she wanted to feel that way now. Fuck Gretchen! Fuck her and her candy-ass lovers (she was thinking of Chandra, who was more ladylike than most of their friends) and her country house. Leni was pleased at "candy ass," an expression she had just heard recently. She worked up her rage, digging in the shovel, lifting the dirt to drop at the low end of the floor. Damn right! she muttered, it was better to be digging here in this goddamned basement, using her muscles, than sitting at some goddamned desk taking orders from some goddamned prick.

But after six hours, Leni left a note telling Barbara she was going to make the first day a short one, and she left Barbara's house to walk to the bus. She had become literally incapable of lifting the shovel one more time. Her body was an enormous aching mass that she dragged along, wincing at each jolt of pavement up through her shoe. On the Mission Street bus she flopped down in a seat and let her legs fall open, in the way the teenage boys did, taking up a seat and a half. When someone sat next to them, they did not move, forcing the other rider to perch on one quarter the area of the seat. Her belligerence led her to resolve that if such a teenager sat next to her she would not move her leg. She eased down in the seat, her fatigue making her slightly dizzy. Two stops later, she watched a rough-looking boy approaching down the aisle, and realized the seat next to her was the only one empty. The young man sat down. Leni did not bring her legs any closer together, forcing him to sit on the outer edge of the seat. But he shoved in farther and opened his legs, his thigh in its neatly ironed black chino pressing against Leni's dirt-caked fatigue pants. Still she did not move her leg, and they rode down Mission Street with their thighs glued together, neither looking at each other or acknowledging this hostile intimacy.

When she got off the bus, Leni hobbled to the corner grocery
to buy two cans of beer. In the apartment she threw herself on
the mattress in the middle room and began to drink the beer,
and she waited for Windstone's call. For no reason either she or
Windstone could understand, Windstone felt a compelling urge
to communicate with Leni every day. She usually called at dinner time, and Leni was always happy to hear her voice.

"I'm dead," Leni said to her now on the phone. "I've been
digging ditches all day."

"Don't you think it'll get easier when you get used to it?"
Windstone asked.

"I don't think I'm strong enough. My body feels like it's going to pieces."

"Get in a hot bath," Windstone advised. "Soak for a while
and then eat dinner and you'll feel better."

"You're a friend."

"You bet I am, Leni." And Windstone laughed.

"Do you really think I can do that work?"

"What do *you* think?"

Leni sat up straighter and drained her beer. "Well, I found
out I like it better than sitting at a typewriter."

"Then you can do it."

They talked then about when they would see each other on
the weekend. This was always a complicated topic, as Windstone had four other lovers. She saw them at varying intervals,
some once or twice a month, others at weekly junctures. Pa-
tiently she had explained to Leni that by lovers she did not
mean the kind of exclusive and all-consuming relationship that
Leni had had with Gretchen. Windstone made love with her
friends. Far from being an escape from intimacy, the usual ex-
planation for nonmonogamy, Windstone's having many lovers
was a multiplying of emotional as well as sexual intimacy. She
tried to be scrupulously responsible to each woman, working
hard to manage her complicated schedule so that no one would
feel hurt or rejected. Leni was impressed, and secretly she was
relieved, for if Windstone was so busily occupied elsewhere she
would not ask too much of Leni or imagine that their sleeping
together had some particular significance.

They settled on Saturday night, and Windstone asked Leni if
they could spend all day Saturday together. Leni said yes, thinking there was a lot she could learn from Windstone, who always
seemed to know what she wanted and how to ask for it.

After her hot bath, Leni ate a sandwich and then crawled into
bed, pulling the covers around her, settling her aching body as
best she could. She was not at all sure that she would be able to
go to Barbara's in the morning, but the thought left her as she
plunged into sleep.

That night, for the first time in a month, Leni slept the whole
night through, oblivious of the circus going on in the next apartment.

* * *

It made sense that the family next door had not moved out,
Leni thought as she sat on the Mission Street bus the next morning. She had been foolish, at the retreat, to imagine they would
be gone when she came home. If she were that woman, she
would not move out. She would stay until the landlord took le-
gal action, which might not happen for months.

So there would be no change at home, Leni realized, and for
a few minutes she let herself contemplate the idea she had formulated at the retreat—of finding another place to live, a room
even. She had imagined quiet, a window looking out on green-
ness. But Leni knew she wasn't ready. For now she wanted to
stay in the apartment where she and Gretchen had lived their
joint lives, she wanted still to feel Gretchen's presence in the
rooms, or to sense her absence with an immediacy made more intense by the sight of her things.

That day Leni worked on a patch of basement floor too hard
packed to shovel. She had to use a pickaxe to break up the dirt,
swinging the pick high, bringing it down, following with her
body, lifting it high again. When a small area was broken into
clods, Leni picked up the shovel to move the dirt to the lower
end. Then she went back to work with the pickaxe. By afternoon her back and arms throbbed with pain, but she made herself continue for seven hours. On the bus ride home, she felt as

if all her sense organs had stopped functioning, as if she were a corpse propped there with her head lolling against the greasy windowpane.

Again she slept the whole night through.

On Friday evening, Leni wrote in her notebook:

Last night it felt like I hit bottom. Gretchen called me in the evening and she just mentioned she'd been in town the night before to hear Judy Chicago talk at the Art Institute. Well, that made me feel like shit, that she'd come to the same town with me and not even given me a call, and then I realized she must have been with Polly. And then she was telling me she's so fired up by Judy Chicago's Dinner Party project that she's going down to L.A. for a week in March to help work on it. I told her I thought that was terrific, and then I realized that she's going in the month that Polly will be down there. So I mentioned Polly and she said, Oh well, yes, she'll be there—as if that couldn't matter less to her. Then she talked about how her parents might be coming up to stay with her this weekend and her old friend from L.A. is coming up the weekend of the 24th probably. And I felt like she was calling to tell me about all the people she's inviting into her life right now, while I'm not even someone she'll call when she comes to the same town with me.

She tells me I talk too much, that I take up too much space. I begin to feel that I'm too big for her, too much person, too much energy, too many concerns and wanting to communicate. I feel like I have to try to be smaller than I am when I'm with her.

But I want her so much still. I wish I could just dump that. I wish I could get inside myself so firmly that I wouldn't even remember her. But her phone call brought her crashing into my life. It hasn't been long enough, I guess. Really, it's a trip to realize it's been less than two weeks. How awful if this is going to go on for months.

On Sunday, sitting cozily in her bed while rain streamed on the windows, Leni wrote in her notebook:

Things are developing between me and Windstone, though I'm being real careful not to lean into it or make demands. I let her choose, mostly. Adrian says Windstone is a prince who moves through the world choosing people, giving only as much as she wishes. And there is something sort of princely about Windstone.

She's got such a strong hold on herself. It's not that scrappy, tough fighting spirit like Gretchen's. It's just this confidence, like she's serenely sure of herself, and that's probably because her life's been a lot easier than Gretchen's or mine. But whatever it's from, she's quite a person, with a real formidable strength and resolve.

But I've discovered she <u>does</u> play some little games with all these lovers she has. She told me one of them was mad at her because she'd been seeing a lot of her before the retreat and then afterwards Windstone had just pulled away and not even called her. She admitted that's a pattern she has, to get scared and pull away, and I said, Are you warning me? and she said, I guess so.

So she arranged to spend today with that woman and had to get up out of bed with me this morning at 8:30 and go out into a steady rain to drive back over to Oakland. I wondered how I'd feel when she was gone, but I feel fine now. I'm glad to be alone here writing in this notebook, eating breakfast in bed.

Yesterday was beautiful. Windstone and I went out into my neighborhood, first to the candle store around the corner on Valencia. A voodoo sort of place, all musty and dark. We both bought large candles just the shade of my blue bedroom walls. Then we went to Old Wives Tales to pick up the copy of "Cold Comfort Farm" I had ordered after Adrian told me it was really funny. At Rainbow Grocery we got the fruit for a big salad Windstone wanted to make. She told me she really likes my neighborhood, and I felt so good seeing her enjoy it so much. It was a healing thing for me, since Gretchen had been so down on this neighborhood, so snotty to me for being happy here. I saw that Windstone really knows how to be right here where she is and have a good time, though sometimes she resists this, maybe because she thinks that simple happiness is too humble for an exalted creature like herself.

We took the fruit salad out in the side lot, in the sun. Smoked a little dope and sat in the grass eating the salad. Got very still. And I was perfectly happy. Watched a small snail climb a grass blade, shell transparent, neck glistening in the sun, antenna waving. Birds were singing. That beautiful fat little baby that lives on the third floor in the back house waved to us from the window. I knew that Windstone was as quiet as I was. We were supposed to go to the beach, but she leaned over to me and said I love it here, I would almost rather stay here than go to the beach. And I felt

so comforted by her, that she could like my apartment and my
backyard and be content there.

Later when we came back from the beach we decided we felt
so free there because that ocean and huge sky were big enough
for us. We could just keep expanding without getting in anyone's
way.

* * *

Gradually, Leni's body began to adjust to her work. While she
was still deeply tired each afternoon when she rode the bus home,
her muscles did not ache so acutely, and she knew her strength
was increasing. She and Barbara were still working in the basement, where Leni tore up some old flooring, carried great chunks
of broken concrete to pile in the backyard, cut off the rotting
floor supports with an electric saw, dug holes for pier blocks.
Part of the task, she discovered, was being careful. So far she had
not injured herself seriously, although one day she stepped on a
loose board and did a quick Charlie Chaplin flip to land straddling
some floor supports fearing her leg was broken. For a few moments she panicked, for Barbara had gone off and Leni was alone
in the house. But then as she gingerly examined her leg she found
it was only bruised, and when she could breathe again she pulled
herself up and went back to work. Her hands were scratched now,
and calluses had begun to form on her palms.

Still, she liked the work, used it to release her anger, escaped
into it to avoid her sadness. She liked challenging her body, and
feeling rough. And she liked getting filthy, her clothes and skin
covered with dirt, her body pungent with sweat.

Sometimes she felt guilty that she was not just now working
on some political project, but she was too tired each evening to
want to do more than drink beer, talk to Windstone on the telephone, and go to bed.

Her feelings for Gretchen fluctuated madly, but she had decided that she wanted to stay in contact with Gretchen, no matter how much it hurt. She did not want to do what her husband
had done, sacrificed their whole relationship because she would
not live with him as his wife. Gretchen had never been her wife
or her husband. She and Gretchen were two *women* who loved

each other no matter what living arrangements they might make. She determined she would not give in to her anger and hurt by rejecting Gretchen.

On Valentine's Day, Gretchen called her, and they began to argue.

"I can *tell* you why I don't want to be lovers with you now. Look at it this way. If we were lovers, would you be able to go to a dance and see me there with Polly and be accepting of that and feel all right about it?"

"No, I would feel jealous and rejected."

"You have no right to feel that way!" Gretchen's angry voice insisted. "It's my life and Polly's life. It has nothing to do with you."

"Still, I would feel hurt and rejected."

"Well, that's one reason I don't want to be lovers with you, because you won't work with your jealousy or go beyond it."

Leni simply listened, sitting in the green kitchen looking at the posters on the wall.

"And besides that," Gretchen went on, "I am not physically attracted to you."

That stung. Leni felt her equanimity desert her.

"I feel pushed around by you sexually. I don't like that intense sexuality that you want. My rhythm is slower and less demanding."

Leni twisted the telephone cord. "You used to like it fine."

"Well, I've changed. I wish you'd realize that."

Leni was silent.

"Did you send me a Valentine's Day present?" Gretchen asked.

Leni couldn't believe she had heard correctly.

"What?"

"A Valentine's Day present, I sent *you* one. You probably didn't even think about it, right?"

Leni slammed her hand down on the table. "For Christ's sake!"

"See, you say you care about me but you really don't!"

And suddenly Leni found herself laughing. "Oh Gretchen, do you realize how ridiculous that sounds?!"

"Huh?"

"Valentine's Day. Hearts and flowers. *Come on!*" And Leni went on chortling uncontrollably. She felt Gretchen's silence at the other end, and then she felt it break.

"Okay, it's silly," Gretchen said meekly. "Hearts and flowers, why not?" And then she too was laughing.

And then she said, "You actually *like* this fighting, don't you Leni."

"Well," Leni admitted, ". . . sometimes. It's better . . . it's better than your feeling sorry for me. I know you resent me, and I don't want you to patronize me by being nicey-nicey to me. At least when we fight we're *equals.*"

They talked then for a time as friends, bruised by each other but caring strongly nevertheless.

* * *

In her notebook Leni wrote:

Dream Wednesday morning maybe from reading "Cold Comfort Farm" the night before. On a farm, me and a woman lover. I am the newcomer. Our small house is almost like a hallway, with other people tramping through at all hours. I'm real upset by this, feel invaded. And when I try to talk to my lover about it, she acts as if it's perfectly natural. Frustration.

Windstone asked me what it meant to me, and I realized I felt this way about Gretchen's and my relationship. All that used to be so private and protected by us—now she's letting other people in there—to walk through, make their judgments. She doesn't value what we had or want to protect it anymore.

Crying then. Grief at this loss.

* * *

A few days later, Leni and Windstone fought. Windstone had spent the weekend at a retreat in Berkeley of women healers and therapists set up to bring about a deepening understanding between white and Third World women. The conference exploded into a heated confrontation that took the women to the brink of violence. One of the white women who had been most traumatized by the fight was Windstone's lover Karen. Windstone called Leni to break the date she and Leni had arranged, saying she was going to stay in Berkeley to take care of Karen. Leni was furious, Windstone upset and defensive. Windstone said she had assumed Leni would agree that she had to "stay with the reality" of the situation there. Leni shouted that she was tired of this nonmonogamy bullshit. "If you make a date with me you keep it, or else!"

"I'm surprised at you, Leni," Windstone said. "Karen needs me a lot more than you do right now."

Leni raged at her. "Oh yeah, you divide yourself up—a little for this person, a little for that. Well, I'm not up for it."

There was a strained silence, and then Windstone's voice came clogged with disappointment and pain.

"I thought you would understand . . . ."

When Leni put down the phone, she hardened herself against Windstone's distress. And she made the resolve that work would be the center of her life, independent of all relationships. She talked to herself about changing her expectations of Windstone. Then she wondered how it was possible not to become dependent upon the caring and company of someone, when you spent time together, shared so much.

On March 1, Leni wrote in her notebook:

> Yesterday I found out that the little apartment across the street from Barbara's is vacant. It feels like the right place for me to move to. Now, how will I get the money together for the last month's rent and security and cleaning deposit!
>
> I came home and looked around the apartment here, and it all came back to me, those four years with Gretchen, all the love that was here between us, the fun we had. I started to sob and wandered up and down the hall crying. Finally I called Gretchen, and she understands because it's hard for her too. She's having a hard time right now, says her weight's way down, and that wrenches me, makes me feel protective of her, which I hate feeling.
>
> She says she wants to come and help me move, if I get the apartment, and that seems only fair since I helped her move and since so much of the stuff here is hers and will have to be stored someplace. She thinks maybe it will be a good way for us to see each other

again, that we can go through whatever feelings we have to and
maybe even make it a joyful occasion.

But Leni did not get the apartment. The landlord told her his
wife insisted he not rent to a single woman. Leni was working
on the roof of Barbara's house now, fitting and hammering shingles, and she could see the apartment house across the street as
she worked. Now and then she stopped to stare at it, concocting
fantasies of suing the landlord for discrimination. She would
drag him into court and humiliate him, force him to rent her
that crummy little box of an apartment. Carefully, she spread
gooey black tar along the edge of the roof, fitted the metal flash-
ing over it, and nailed it in place, watching the tar ooze out from
under it. She knew she had neither time nor money to take the
landlord to court. She was beginning to worry about money
now, and about finding a place to live since she had given notice
to Mr. Chiu.

Leni realized, ironically, that she would probably move before
the family next door moved, and she thought, well, perhaps that
was fitting. Their noise bothered her less now than it had. Partially she was becoming accustomed to it, but she also recognized that she had been in a particularly shaky and vulnerable
condition in January, and the noise from next door had seemed
only another violation.

Leni wrote in her notebook:

A hard time with Windstone letting her know how I felt about
our fight. She agreed to take me more into account next time
something like this comes up. She'll try to give me more notice
and spend more time talking with me about it. Finally I felt all
right again and so did she.

So then we got into smoking dope and eating popcorn, sitting
in her kitchen, and Windstone told me about this trapeze class she
just started, where she fell on her head, which I thought was funny
and she did not. And then she was working on my neck and shoulders, loosening me up so much that I could hardly stand up or walk.
We went to bed and were very close. Windstone was being affectionate and sensual. She was making love in the way she sometimes
defines it, not genitally but with her whole body and self, much
stroking and cradling, very slow and easeful and delicious. Funny

how much I had resisted this when we were first together. I always
went right for genital sex to get the fastest, biggest orgasm possible.
Seems weird to me now that I could not have wanted this slow
sensuality. It's real subtle and gentle. But she had to resist me and
say no, she had to frustrate me for a long time before I could relax
and just let myself be there for whatever might happen between us.
I think I'm lucky she didn't just give up on me and run away.

Working with the wood chisel yesterday at Barbara's. Something really satisfying in that. Then, sanding front door frame.
Putting spackling paste in the grooves. Painting the trim where
it's dirty or stained by moisture. A steady rain keeps me from
working on the roof.

On the bus going over to Barbara's I stood, looking back down
the aisle at the faces. Filipino, Latino, Anglo, Black. Faces seamed
and gouged with years of work and struggle, faces dulled. The
damage done to these human beings, the limitations on what they've
been allowed to become. Felt a great tenderness and sorrow. For
them, for myself.

* * *

In the second week of March, on a Saturday morning, Gretch-
en came to visit. She had to be in the city, she told Leni: could
they spend some time together?

That morning Leni sat in the kitchen drinking coffee, the caf-
feine bringing her to a pitch of anxiety. Before her on the table
was the Olga Broumas book, *Beginning with O.* Leni was trying
to read a particular poem; she said the words to herself but no
matter how hard she tried to concentrate, the totality of herself
was engaged in dreading and longing for Gretchen's arrival,
clenched in listening for the doorbell. At its harsh Rrrrrrng, she
got up, dropping the book, and she felt her stomach go liquid.
I'm going to have diarrhea, she thought, as she walked down the
long hall to the door.

She opened the door and stepped out to open the gate, and
then for a few moments she stood motionless in bewilderment,
for there behind the iron latticework stood two young women
in skirts and shapeless coats, smiling eagerly at her.

"Good morning!"

Leni opened the gate and stood back to let them in.

"Good morning," one of them said again, and she handed Leni a small folded sheet of paper. Leni took it, staring confusedly at the more aggressive of the two women, who was talking now, asking Leni if she went to church, if she had found god, if she had a few moments this morning to talk with them about the words of Jesus.

Leni backed up into her own doorway, and there she stood nodding in confusion, aware that her lips were stretched in a silly half smile.

Then, past the shoulders of the two women, she saw Gretchen come in the gate. This much thinner Gretchen was dressed in a red jacket Leni had never seen before. Her hair looked shiny and newly washed. And she was obviously frightened.

Gretchen's eyes, dark and very wide open, met Leni's. They looked at each other past the distance of those six weeks' absence.

The voice of the woman with the pamphlets droned on, as if in a dream.

"No thanks, no thanks," Leni said, and opened her front door wide as Gretchen came around the surprised women.

Leni shut the door, blotting out their faces.

She and Gretchen stood in the hallway.

"You look really good," Gretchen said quickly.

Leni felt as if her face were crumbling in layers under the skin. She turned away to hide it.

"New jacket?" she asked.

"I was hoping you'd like it," Gretchen said. "It's a new style for me. I found it in a thrift shop." And she held out her arm for Leni to examine.

Leni was able to turn then and look. The red coat was softer and more dressy than most of Gretchen's clothes. And its color livened her dark skin.

"Pretty," Leni said. "Really nice."

"Yeah."

They stood a few feet from each other in the shadowy hall, and neither knew what to do next. Gretchen took a deep breath, slapped her sides with her arms, and said, "Well."

Leni went past her then. "Come on down to the kitchen."
It felt extremely strange to be inviting Gretchen into this kitch-
en which had been hers for four years.

They sat on opposite sides of the table in the green room.
Leni looked at Gretchen, and she knew every hollow and swelling of her body under the clothes, every odor, taste, every expression of face and hands. This was excruciating: how expos-
ing it was to know so much.

"See?" Leni said quickly. "You remember this book I was
looking for—the Olga Broumas one?" She picked up the book,
holding it for Gretchen to see. "Well, I found it . . . ." And she
began leafing through it to find the particular poem she had
been reading.

Gretchen's silence made Leni glance up at her face, which was
sorrowing and amused at the same time. "Will you put that
down, Leni, and sit next to me?"

Leni held the book before her for a few moments more, looking at Gretchen, and then she put it down.

Gretchen reached across the table to stroke her face, cupping
her hand on Leni's cheek.

"It's so good to see you."

Leni moved to sit next to her, and they began to touch each
other, face and shoulders and hair, their hands tentative, careful.
Gretchen turned Leni's hand palm upwards, placing her own
next to it. "Hey, twin calluses. You've become a manual labor-
er, like me." And she bent to kiss Leni's palm.

Leni looked down at Gretchen's thick black hair, at the
streaks of grey shining like the striations in rock. And when
Gretchen sat up straight again they kissed very gently. Then
they sat holding each other for a long time, their eyes closed.
And Leni felt as she had in those first weeks she had known
Gretchen, when in their being together it had seemed she was
coming home.

They talked then, and Leni told Gretchen about the place in
the Berkeley Hills she had heard about. It was a room in a
house where many women's movement activists had lived. She
had an appointment to go see it next week.

"You mean you'd consider moving to Berkeley?" Gretchen's voice was heavy with sarcasm.

"Yes. I'm willing to try it now, if I like that place and can get it. Adrian told me there's a big backyard and trees, and a view of the Golden Gate Bridge from that room. And it's cheap."

"Dammit!" Gretchen turned her head away. "*Now*, when I'm not *here*, you're willing to move to Berkeley."

She looked at Leni, and Leni saw her struggling.

"I should be furious!"

"I feel differently about a lot of things now," Leni said defensively.

Gretchen shook her head. "Leni Clare in Berkeley? Well, I never!" And she rolled her eyes. "What will that do to your image?"

Leni closed her lips tightly.

Later, they went to eat lunch at a vegetarian restaurant, where Gretchen wanted to tell Leni about Polly and Chandra and a new lover named Muriel. Leni shook her head.

"But I want to share with you what I'm learning in relationships," Gretchen said earnestly. "So much I wish I had known when I was with you."

Leni felt herself close up inside. "Don't tell me about your lovers."

Gretchen watched her. "Yes. All right. I'm sorry. I guess it's too soon."

And when she asked, "How are you and Windstone getting along?" Leni answered only "Fine."

It was Gretchen's idea that they should go shopping together, but in the first store Leni was stricken with a headache so brutal it nauseated her. When they finally got back to the apartment, she had to go to bed. And irony thickened as Gretchen fixed dinner for her, once more having to take care of her. Leni apologized. She felt awful.

That night she was aware of Gretchen's body there beside her, though at first she was protected even from thoughts of intimacy by the headache. Later, Gretchen sighed and turned in her sleep, in a movement so known to Leni that she felt stretched on a grid of hot wires. In the middle of the night she could not help herself: she reached to touch Gretchen's hair. "What? What?" Gretchen mumbled, startling awake, and jerked away from Leni's hand, muttering, "No . . . so tired . . ." and went immediately back to sleep. Leni didn't dare touch her again. This was so little like the way they used to sleep closely entwined, used to awaken each morning together, drift back to sleep for a few minutes with their faces touching, arms around each other.

In the bright morning after the night of restless waking, Leni was wracked with feelings deep and contradictory.

Gretchen, getting dressed, told her about the ritual to be led by Chandra that morning in Berkeley. It was a ritual designed to deal with fear of nuclear war, to release the dread and horror, and show people a way to channel their concern into action. Gretchen was sure it would be powerful, Chandra had been working so hard on it. "You're welcome to come if you like," she said, buttoning her shirt before the mirror.

"Oh, *thank* you *so much!*"

Gretchen turned in surprise to look at Leni.

"I can come there with all your other lovers," Leni said. "Won't that be fun."

Gretchen frowned. "This is not a *date* with Chandra. She probably won't even talk to me, she'll be so busy."

"Oh yeah? I'll bet she'll sneak in something."

Gretchen stared at her. "What's this about, Leni?"

Leni raised up on her knees in bed, lifting her fist. "It's about how you make me feel!"

"But I'm just inviting you to come with me."

"Oh yeah, the afterthought—why not take good old Leni along. Will Polly and Muriel and Donna be there too? What a great foursome . . . ."

Gretchen interrupted in a harsh, furious voice. "You think you have such a hard time. You think people *make* you *feel bad*. Why don't you take responsibility for your own feelings. Why don't you understand that nobody has it any easier! You're just like some big baby wanting everyone to take care of you. Grow up, Leni!"

And Leni started to cry. She told Gretchen how excluded she felt that Gretchen and Chandra had shared the preparations for this event, and now she, Leni, was casually invited to the finished product. She felt once again how completely Gretchen had shut her out of her life.

"Dammit, Leni, why can't you get *past* this? I said it that way because I didn't know if you'd *want* to come. And why do we have to fight now? I was *afraid* this would happen."

"Because I have *feelings*!" Leni screamed. "I have some feelings about all this. Don't you?! Are you really that detached?"

"I wish you would use a little restraint," Gretchen said. "We're due in Berkeley in half an hour, if you're going."

"I'm just trying to tell you how I feel! Is that against the rules? Are people not supposed to do that?"

"Look, why don't you stay here. I'll go by myself."

"Yes, that's a good idea."

When Gretchen was halfway out the door, Leni called out, "Are you coming back here after?"

Gretchen had settled the floppy black hat on her head, and she spoke from under its brim. "No, I'm heading back up to the country. Goodbye."

That afternoon Leni took a long walk up Dolores Street where the palm trees sparkled in the sun. When she came in the house, the phone was ringing. She ran for the kitchen and picked up the receiver, breathless.

"Hi," Gretchen's voice said.

"Hello."

"I'm about to take off for Guerneville. Thought I'd see how you're doing."

"I took a walk. I feel better."

"Good. I've decided I don't want to do that kind of thing anymore—just walk out."

"No?"

"No. Hey, I missed you this afternoon. I wish you'd been able to come along."

Leni said nothing.

"I've got to go now," Gretchen's voice came. "I just want you to know I still love you, Leni."

When Leni put down the phone she sat for a long time in the kitchen. The cat came to curl in her lap and she stroked it, remembering how she and Gretchen had sat here yesterday, touching each other.

* * *

On Tuesday she stood in a room in Berkeley, looking out its windows to the distant red span of Golden Gate Bridge, the clustered buildings of San Francisco across the flat shining waters of the Bay. When she looked down she saw roofs of the elegant old houses in among the trees, extending down the hill to the flats of Berkeley and Albany. And here just below the window was a sloping yard surrounded by trees, in which stood a white-painted picnic table and bench. The height of these windows, the enormous view, from Oakland on the left all the way to Mt. Tamalpais on the right, made Leni feel as if she were floating in space. There was none of that sense of packed humanity that she was used to, but a serene solitude. She gazed out across the rooftops, the water glittering in the sun, where a tiny white sailboat leaned, and she felt a great rush of excitement. Could she live here? And the answer came, yes. Yes, it would be like living in a sanitarium, away from real life, for a while. And she was ready for that. The last few months had finished her on the Mission district, the unrelenting chaos in the apartment next door had been too much to tolerate. She wanted to escape it. Live up here with the rich folks? Well, that would be a little odd, but she was ready to try it. And what of that sense of all those lives crowded around her, that reassuring mass of humanity? Leni realized that there had been a loneliness within her, especially during the years when she had been married; she had needed that proximity to others in order to ease the loneliness. Now, she realized, that sense of isolation was no longer present in her; her connection with other human beings was felt, a certainty in herself that did not depend on the physical closeness of others. Or so she formulated this, standing at the window, and she thought, I want to see how I'll be, living here, looking out at all this open space. I want to see what it will do to my mind.

Leni went downstairs to talk with Diana and Kathleen, the women who lived in the house. The three of them sat in the spacious living room with its fireplace and windows looking out on trees, and Kathleen explained the situation. "It's pretty unusual for any of these houses up here to be rented, but there are a few, like this one, where the owner is an old woman who raised her family here and holds onto the house for sentimental reasons. Our landlady lives in an apartment house in San Francisco, and she hasn't really paid attention to the rise in property values over here, which is why our rent is so cheap."

Diana was a large, fresh-faced woman in overalls and tie-dyed T-shirt who reminded Leni a little of Windstone. Kathleen looked to be about forty years old, with greying short-cropped hair and sharp blue eyes that watched Leni attentively.

"Do you live collectively here?"

Diana shook her head. "Not really right now. Kathleen and I both just recently escaped from heavy communal situations. So we're taking a break from that. We share expenses and sometimes we eat together, but generally we live *around* each other."

Leni questioned them, discovering that Diana was a lesbian and Kathleen, who defined herself as heterosexual, had been celibate for two years. They questioned her, and she told them about her previous political work. They had mutual friends, they discovered, and soon they were talking about women's movement politics in the Bay Area in the last five years. Kathleen and Diana were both active in a group working to combat violence against women as it is portrayed in pornography, television, movies. Kathleen told Leni they were particularly concerned about the portrayal of Third World women as victims, and she described some recent actions the group had taken.

When she walked down the hill to the bus that afternoon, Leni was thrilled. The house seemed the perfect place for her to move to. She liked the women, Kathleen especially, and she could imagine working with them politically. The rent was low, and, incredibly, they asked no last month's rent or security. Now they had to make their decision, for they told her several women were already interested in the place. She was to call them on the weekend to find out.

Leni rode the bus across Berkeley and into Oakland to Windstone's house throbbing with excitement, yet afraid to want this too much.

"I'm ready for the change, I think!" she told Windstone.

Windstone hugged her. "Leni, I'm so proud of you. Oh I hope you get it. You'll be on *my* side of the *Bay*!"

That night as they ate dinner in Windstone's tiny wood-panelled kitchen, Leni watched her. With her bright eyes, her strong jaw in a clean-lined face, her hair cut smooth and short, Windstone was a fresh young Amazon. Leni felt in herself how much she liked Windstone's eagerness, her brashness. And what had seemed at first a discouraging gulf in their class backgrounds had turned into an advantage in their relationship. Windstone's growing up in a middle-class family, where she was given a great deal, including expensive educational trips to Europe, had led her to believe that she could have what she wanted in the world, an attitude very much unlike Leni's working class conviction that nothing would ever come her way. Leni found it heartening to be with someone who was so calmly confident. When she had been with Gretchen, Leni's and Gretchen's similar backgrounds had been a source of understanding between them, but sometimes by their conviction of not being good enough, their experience that life was difficult, rewards uncertain and hard won, they had dragged each other down. Then the Mickey Rooney pep talks were empty words, neither one of them really believing that things could get better. Windstone gave Leni another perspective on the world. Leni had never been with someone who said, simply, I want that (without fear, denial or conflict), and then moved confidently to get it. She watched Windstone, amazed.

* * *

That Friday at Barbara's house, Barbara sat on the porch with Leni while Leni ate her lunch. "You've done great here," she said. "I've loved working with you and having you in my house."

Leni put down her sandwich, knowing what was coming and wondering whether she would be sad or happy when she heard it.

"I'm running out of money," Barbara said, opening her hands. "I went through my accounts last night and I realized I don't

have a dollar more to spend on remodelling. So I'm going to
have to stop right here."

"Well . . . ."

"Would it hang you up really bad if we made this your last
day? I know I should have given you notice, but I hadn't looked
at my money until last night . . . ."

Leni took a deep breath, feeling light-headed. "It could be
perfect," she said. "It just might be exactly right."

That afternoon Barbara wrote out the last check, and she
laughed uncomfortably. "Well, if nothing else, you oughta
know how to build your own house now."

Leni hugged her. "Cross your fingers for me that I get that
room in Berkeley, will you?"

As she left the house, she turned to look at it, and she realized
she felt differently about that small yellow frame house than she
had about any other. Through her labor it was strengthened, repaired, protected. She knew its contours and spaces with her
body in a way that was somehow more intimate than any house
she had inhabited. She was fond of that house, she realized.
Maybe she'd come back and see it one day.

On the bus ride home, she felt both satisfied and disoriented.
Leni liked activities and environments to remain the same. Now,
suddenly everything in her life seemed either to have shifted or
be on the edge of change. She felt lifted off the ground.

But at home there were Gretchen's plants to water, Gretchen's
matted prints on the wall. There was the cat to feed and pet, a
beer to drink. And Windstone would call her soon. This at
least, for the moment, held steady.

From next door came the sound of loud talking as the oldest
girl harangued her brothers and sisters. Listening as she sat at
the kitchen table, Leni thought how that mother and her children could not escape to a gracious old house in the Berkeley
Hills. When they were kicked out of here one day, they might
be able to move to the great square crowded box of the projects,
or they might wind up in another too small apartment in an aged
Victorian apartment house, if they were lucky. Leni wondered
if there might have been anything she could have done to help,
and thought, yes, probably so, if she had not been so upset her-

self with Gretchen's leaving; and she felt acutely the inequity between herself and the woman next door.

The next day Leni paced the hallway from the living room all
the way back to the kitchen. She stood over the phone, uncertain. Diana and Kathleen at the Berkeley house had said, Call on
the weekend. Was Saturday afternoon too early? Should she
wait until evening? She walked up the hallway again and
stopped at the front door. Through the wall came the usual hub-
bub and music from next door. She stood listening to it for a
few minutes, looking into the front room at Gretchen's plants.
So much of the furniture in the apartment was Gretchen's. In
fact, almost all of it. What to do about *that*? Leni went down
the hall to the kitchen again, and this time put her hand on the
phone. Go ahead, she told herself. Just say, I wondered if you
had made your decision yet. Or you can say, Hi, this is Leni.
Who gets the room? No, that's too flip, as if you didn't care.
She sat down at the table, got up again, and went to the sink to
wash up yesterday's dishes. Then, wiping her hands on a dish-
towel, she wondered if she ought to scrub the kitchen floor. She
could call after that. But no.

Leni looked at the number written on a piece of paper on the
kitchen table, picked up the phone and dialed, saying in her
mind, I just wondered if . . . . A busy signal buzzed flatly in
her ear.

Busy! They must be offering it to someone else! Leni put
down the phone, her stomach tingling.

She scrubbed the floor, assuring herself that they could be
talking on the phone about *anything*. Political people, she reminded herself, always spend a lot of time on the phone.

She called again. Busy.

It was evening, and Windstone had just arrived for their date
when the phone rang in Leni's kitchen.

"That's *them*!" Leni said breathlessly, and she clung to Windstone.

"So answer it Leni."

The voice was clearly Kathleen's. "We've decided," she said
evenly, "that we'd like you to move in if you're still interested."

Leni and Windstone hopped around the kitchen screeching
with joy.

"I'm gonna get a bottle of wine to celebrate!"

Windstone shrugged. She did not drink alcohol, and while
she never objected to Leni's drinking, she did not encourage it.

Leni went out to walk to the store. On her way there and
back, she looked at the house fronts, at the litter on the sidewalks, at the people, some so raw and beaten looking, and she
thought, soon, for a little while, I won't be here to see this, I
won't be part of it, victim to it. And she knew every foot of
that block and a half from her door to the grocery store would
remain in her, no matter where she lived.

That night she drank too much and talked Windstone into going to A Little More, one of the biggest of the women's bars, to
dance.

The next evening, when Windstone had gone home, Leni
called Gretchen's number in the country.

"Hi, what's up?" Gretchen's voice was brisk.

"Is someone with you?"

"Yes."

"I'll just take a minute."

"Oh, it's all right."

When Leni told her she would soon move to Berkeley, Gretch-
en said, "Oh yeah, that's terrific," but her voice was empty of
interest.

"I wanted to know how we'll deal with all your things. It's
just a room I'm moving to, and all I'll need will be the bed and
desk."

"Oh . . . ." Leni felt Gretchen struggling to concentrate.
"Well, I'll help you move . . . I said I would. And I'll find a
place to store my stuff . . . ."

They made plans for the last weekend in the month, and Leni
hung up the phone. She wondered which of Gretchen's women
was there, and for an hour or so she felt forlorn. It was awful
to talk to Gretchen on the phone when she was distracted.
Much worse than no contact at all. Leni got in bed and read
The Nature of Personal Reality until she was too sleepy to make
out the words, deliberately not thinking of Gretchen, and then
she slept.

In the next week she began moving her things to Berkeley, in Windstone's car, box by box.

On March 20, she wrote in her notebook:

Three days camping at the Yuba River. I was scared to go because I'm moving and I'm out of money, but Windstone talked me into it. You have to live your life money or not, moving or not, she says. I have to guard against worry.

Tarot reading done by Windstone on a flat white rock in the river. Queen of Wands—me. Atmosphere: Page of Cups—new ways of doing, new energy, good aspect; cheerful loving card. The Page is a student, learning new ways, a piscean card, flowing. The Known: Seven of Wands—struggle, difficulty, conflict. The Unknown: Ace of Cups—a gift of something miraculous, water spilling over, the dove bringing a gift.

It was a great reading I thought, because the question I asked was whether I'll be able to be productive in a way I need to be and whether I'll find work in Berkeley.

Windstone says the Queen of Wands is a witch. She transforms things, brings them together, makes new substances from them (that is, making this move what I need it to be).

In the last few days of this month Gretchen comes so we can move all her things out of the San Francisco apartment. When I think of being with her again I can feel a great big space opening inside my chest, like the beach when it's cold and windy. It's echoey in there, and icy and sharp.

But we've got to do this moving together.

I'm a little confused right now. I don't know where I live yet, not in Berkeley quite yet but no longer in San Francisco. And I can't believe it but there's still all that pain and anger and love in me for Gretchen. How to get rid of it, once and for all!

The work at Barbara's house was very good for me, I see now. It demystified the building and fixing process. I found out it's no big deal to saw and hammer and figure out how to make things, and so I've done it easily in my new room. I built in a desk and painted my chair and took the door off the closet. All of it I did without even asking for advice, and that was very good for me.

* * *

It took two days to move all of Gretchen's things from the apartment. On the first morning Leni borrowed Barbara's van, and she and Gretchen loaded it with the furniture and the large items that were Gretchen's. They worked quickly, irritably, snapping at each other, criticizing each other. Gretchen was brusque, admitting no feelings. Leni felt depressed and listless.

They carried out the cedar chest, maneuvered the kitchen table down the long narrow hallway, took the bureau and the sectioned bookcase out the door. Gretchen's face was angry looking, her nose a pale ridge standing out abruptly. In the midst of this heavy work, her eyes rarely met Leni's, except when she shot her a furious glance over the top of a piece of furniture, saying, "Watch what you're *doing*, Leni. You're going to scratch the finish."

The work exhausted them. When they got in the van to drive across the Bay to Berkeley, where Gretchen had found storage space in the garage of a friend, Leni began to cry. She sat wedged in a mesh of chair legs, and let the tears roll down her cheeks, not even bothering to wipe them. Gretchen, who was driving, hunched over the wheel, thrusting her face forward, staring at the road.

When they arrived at the garage, Leni sat in the truck while Gretchen went in the house to talk to her friend. Leni wiped her face with the cloth of her shirt and tried to gather her energy for the unloading. Having vented her grief, she felt detached now, wanting only to finish the task.

This they accomplished in less than an hour. Then Gretchen suggested they go to a mutual friend's to take a hot tub, and in a short time they were in that round redwood enclosure, immersed to their chests in steaming water. The hot tub stood in the fenced back yard of the house. Above it loomed a giant tree, majestic against a darkening sky. From the kitchen of the house, Leni and Gretchen could hear the voice of their friend talking to her daughter.

Leni sank down until the water came to her chin, and breathed deeply of the steam. The heat soothed her aching muscles, and she thought how wonderful it would have been to come home from those first few days of work at Barbara's to a luxury like this.

Although the tub was small, Gretchen and Leni did not touch ankles or knees, careful not to brush against each other as they changed positions, as they sighed and rested their heads back on the rim of the tub, gazing up at the sky. Leni had watched Gretchen lower herself into the water. She had looked at the strong thighs, thinner now, the mound of curly black pubic hair, the breasts with their thick nubs of nipple, and a shudder of tenderness had gone through her. Now she was intensely aware of Gretchen's body, so near to her. And inevitably she thought of the women who made love to Gretchen now.

"So how's your harem these days?" she asked in a falsely casual voice.

"Oh Leni, leave me alone," came Gretchen's tired voice.

"Have you added any new ones since I talked to you last?"

There came a ripple of hot water as Gretchen adjusted herself in the tub.

"Those are real women I am relating to in a real way," she said. "I'm not some man making conquests. I wish you'd acknowledge that."

Leni couldn't help it. She was consumed with desire for Gretchen, and so she said, "Well, Donna, Polly, Chandra, Muriel, that's quite a list."

Gretchen's voice came low and dead sounding. "Donna hasn't been around for a long time."

"What happened? Couldn't take the competition?"

"If you really want to know . . . if you really care . . . Donna, it turns out, was only playing around. Once I was free and available, she wasn't."

"I didn't know that."

"I haven't felt like telling you my business these days. I think it's pretty obvious why."

They were silent then, and Leni looked at Gretchen to find the dark eyes watching her. Little curls of steam rose off the water into the cool night air between them. From the kitchen came the sound of a radio turned low, muttering unintelligibly.

"That must have felt really bad," Leni said finally, sincerely."

Gretchen's look became a hard stare. "Relationships are fucked."

Leni felt great drops of perspiration run down over her temples.

"I will never again have an exclusive relationship with anyone," Gretchen said. "I'll never again give over to anyone like I did to you."

Leni was secretly pleased at Gretchen's bitterness, covertly happy to know that the new love relationships had not all turned out well.

"You *used* me," Gretchen went on. And now her eyelids shielded her eyes. "You used me to get your political work done. For months you locked yourself away inside that struggle, and then when you got fired you disappeared into a depression. And I took care of you."

Leni spread her arms to rest around the curve of the tub, tilted her head back to look up at tree branches against sky.

"You wouldn't hear that *I* was hurting. You didn't *care*," Gretchen said.

Leni brought her arms down into the tub with a splash.

"Goddammit, you never *told* me. You sat and watched TV and wouldn't talk to me!"

"That was after I found out you didn't listen."

"I wish you'd take a little responsibility," Leni said through clenched teeth. "You're a strong woman. That's one of the things I've always liked best about you, that you were tough and knew how to do things. Why didn't you *make* me listen. Why didn't you just say, I'm tired of paying the rent, let's find some other way."

"I was afraid you'd leave me."

"Oh wow, you must have a great idea of who *I* am, to think that."

"It's how I felt," Gretchen said stubbornly.

That evening when they told their friend goodbye and thanked her, they were tight and separate from each other. They drove across town and up the tree-lined, quiet street to which Leni had moved. They entered her house and went upstairs to fall exhausted into bed.

Gretchen rolled over to lie against Leni, but Leni could feel the resistance in her own body. Leni closed her eyes, trying to distance herself from the physical awareness of Gretchen. Almost every night for four years they had held each other; so often the closeness had led to making love. All that knowledge of Gretchen swelled in Leni, hurting. She pulled deep inside herself, looking out the windows to grey clouds that had begun massing in the black sky.

In the morning as they lay quietly next to each other, Gretchen said in a small voice, "I feel like crying." Leni waited. Gretchen sobbed then, all the pain that had been under the bitterness wracking her. Leni watched the rain streaming on the windows.

"Leni, you don't know how I wish I had been able to stay with you." Gretchen's voice was choked. "I still don't know why I had to go off by myself."

Leni held her, feeling her grief.

"Leni, I'm so sorry if I hurt you with those things I said last night in the hot tub. I didn't mean them."

Leni stroked her hair, this hair that she hadn't touched in so long, and something happened in her. Her anger left her in this moment. She wanted only to allow Gretchen to be exactly who she was. Up to now she had thought she *should* do that, but had really wanted to punish and harrass her. Now, understanding, Leni really did *want* to respect her, and saw what freedom there could be for herself in that.

When they got up and dressed, they were wan, shaky at first. "Can we work differently today?" Gretchen asked. "Not rush so? Do it together? Can we?"

Leni was relieved to hear this.

"And maybe when we're finished we can do some kind of ritual to say goodbye to the apartment," Gretchen said.

In pouring rain they drove across the Bay Bridge to the city, made their way to the alley, where Franklin was just coming out the gate.

"Hey, what's goin on?" he asked, standing next to the van with his hands on his hips. "You cuttin' out?"

"Moving to Berkeley," Leni told him.

"That so!" Franklin nodded speculatively. "Well, we'll miss you."

His hair was beaded with moisture, his yellow parka streaming as he went off toward Valencia Street. Leni realized there would be no one like Franklin on her new street in Berkeley, where everyone was white and middle class. And she felt a pang of nostalgia.

At the window of the apartment next door, two small brown faces watched from between the window blind and the glass. But when they saw Leni notice them, they disappeared, leaving the torn blind jiggling.

Leni and Gretchen went through the rain into the building. The apartment was cold and damp in a way it had never been on the coldest day when they had lived there. They were considerate of each other today as they boxed the dishes and silverware, the towels, the books, the hundreds of small objects they had used in their daily living. They worked slowly, and they discussed with each other where the things would go, how they should be packed.

Then they loaded the van, walking out quickly with each box through the rain. When it was full, Gretchen said, "We'll take this over, then make one last trip to get the plants and say goodbye, okay?" This time on the drive to Berkeley Leni did not cry. She drove, looking out the rain-splattered windshield, and when they were safely on the bridge with their cargo, she felt Gretchen move close to her and slip her arm warmly around her shoulders.

Back at the apartment, they brought Gretchen's plants to the van and positioned them carefully. Then they swept each room, scooping the trash into a box, and took the box out to the trash barrels in back.

Both knew it was time then to say goodbye. Gretchen went to the van to get the incense she had brought. She lit two sticks, and gave one to Leni. The faint sweetish odor rose to Leni's nostrils. She followed Gretchen into the front room, and they both stood in silence, not knowing how to begin.

"You want to start?" Gretchen asked.

Leni looked at her. Gretchen's face seemed soft, her eyes very open. Leni took a deep breath and looked around the empty room with its small ugly gas heater, its bay windows.

"This is the room in which Gretchen hung her plants," Leni began, ". . . where she listened to her stereo."

Gretchen picked it up. ". . . where we played sometimes and our friends came and sat around and had fun and met each other."

They did not look at each other. They held their sticks of incense before them, and abruptly, Leni remembered their moving in four years ago, their delight in being together.

"Thank you, room, for making all this possible," Gretchen said.

They went through the sliding doors into the bedroom with its deep blue walls. Leni saw again the yellow drape at the window, like a flash of sunlight. Gretchen had hung it. So many things she had done to bring light and beauty into their lives.

"In this room we lived our most intimate life together," Gretchen said. "Here we slept . . . here we stayed in bed all day and held each other and made love."

It was strange standing in the darkened, empty room. Gretchen's eyes seemed very large as she looked at Leni. They wandered away from each other, came back. And she said, "We'd better not stay in here much longer." Leni nodded. They tried to smile.

"Thank you, room, for sheltering us," Leni said.

And they went down the hall to the bathroom—so bare and white now with all the plants and pictures gone, and the blue shower curtain down. "Thank you, bathroom, for serving us well." Gretchen lingered. "In this tub we took so many baths together."

Leni remembered. The past and the present seemed equally alive here. She felt the strength of their caring as it had been.

And then she looked down at the old tub's lion feet that Gretchen had painted lavender with scarlet toenails, as a joke.

"You were fun to live with," she blurted out, and then was sorry she had spoken so directly, her heart torn as Gretchen said from the doorway, "So were you."

In the middle room they looked at the spot where Leni's desk had sat, the place under the windows where the mattress had lain. Against the opposite wall had stood a cabinet where Gretchen had kept her tools. Leni went to the window opening out into the vacant lot, and she looked up at the flat grey backside of the tenement, behind each window a whole life being lived.

"You really liked it here, didn't you, Leni," Gretchen said from behind her.

Leni turned. "I learned so much."

Gretchen shook her head. "I wish I could have felt that way."

They went to the green-walled kitchen, and Leni stood weighted with the remembrance of all the dinners cooked, all those hours of sitting at the table intently talking to each other. She looked at the pale rectangles on the walls where the posters had hung, and glanced above the sink, remembering the bulletin board with its clusters of notes from friends, like ruffled feathers sticking out. "Gretchen and Leni," they all began—"Leni and Gretchen"—those names in tandem, somehow comprising a unit.

Behind Leni, Gretchen was saying, "Thank you, room, for welcoming our friends who came to dinner or parties. Thank you for the laughter here."

And they were finished. They left the incense burning in the rooms, said a final goodbye to the whole apartment, went out, closed the door and went through the gate to the sidewalk. In the van driving back across the bridge to Berkeley, it was not necessary to talk. They sat close. Gretchen's arm brushed Leni's.

* * *

Three days later, Leni wrote in her notebook:

Friday put me in a really quiet, deep place in myself, and I stayed there all through the weekend when I was being with Windstone and other people. Now this morning, alone in my room, I'm going over what Gretchen and I did, feeling it again.

It took so much more courage than our bitterness. I guess that day we were as large as we've ever been, and I guess we cared about each other as much as we ever will.

She did not write how as they sat in the van in front of her new house that Friday, before taking in the plants, Gretchen had told Leni she was thinking of moving back to the Bay Area. "You know I love it up there for the trees and quiet, but it's too isolated. By the fall I'll be ready to plunge back into life down here." Leni was not surprised. She watched the rain, and rested, waiting because she could feel that Gretchen had more to say.

"And I thought . . . ," Gretchen hesitated. "I wondered if maybe you might want . . . if maybe we might want to live together again."

Leni turned to look at her, her eyes opening wide. Gretchen glanced at her briefly and then lowered her gaze.

"That really shocks me."

Gretchen said nothing. The arch of her nose had gone white.

"Why would you want to?" Leni asked.

Gretchen shrugged, hesitated, and then turned to look full at Leni. "What we had together . . . it was so much deeper than . . . well, than I've found with anyone else. I think now that it was a mistake to leave you."

Leni looked down at her fingers clenched on the door handle. "It's horrible to say that to me."

"Why?"

"Because I have a whole new life now."

"Well, so do I . . . ."

"That's it."

"But . . . ."

"I don't want to talk about this anymore."

"Are you mad at me?

Leni shook her head. "I'm just going to forget you said what you did."

Gretchen shrugged, tapped the steering wheel impatiently, and then she wrenched open the door, letting in the cool wet air.

"Okay, so let's finish up this job," she said.

"Gretchen?"

Her hand on the door, Gretchen stopped, and looked into the van at Leni.

"You're a funny person," Leni said.

Gretchen's body slumped and she leaned on the door as Leni watched a trembling smile open on her lips.

"What I mean . . ." Leni said, ". . . you're my best friend always. That just doesn't change."

Gretchen looked to the side, reached to brush back her hair that was wet now from the rain, and looked back up at Leni.

"Okay," she said. "Okay . . . you mind if we finish this job?"

And she disappeared around the side of the van. Leni sat still for a few moments. She raised a hand to press at her eyes, then leaned her head against the cold glass of window to stare at the wet lawn before her new house. Grass, she said to herself, grass and trees. And she thought how weird and symmetrical their lives were, winding up now one place, now another, where they would never have expected. And somehow still together.